Behold the Man

Soliloquies by Characters
Around Jesus the Day After the Cross

Bobby James Ogdon

SHEILA,
BLESSINGS IN YOUR
SPIRITUAL PILGRIMAGE.

Bobby Ogdon

PublishAmerica
Baltimore

First printing

This is a work of fiction. Names, characters, places, and incidents are the product of the author's imagination or are used fictitiously. Any resemblance to actual persons, living or dead, events, or locales is entirely coincidental.

All Bible quotations are from the New International Version.

ISBN: 1-4241-7772-3
PUBLISHED BY PUBLISHAMERICA, LLLP
www.publishamerica.com
Baltimore

Printed in the United States of America

Table of Contents

Preface

In *Behold the Man*, we read of characters who may have been present as Jesus was crucified at Golgotha, and who, during the next day, reflect upon their relationship with him. The format of soliloquy is a means of self-revelation, allowing us to identify with the speaker and to help us understand the emotional and spiritual responses of these personalities to the death of Our Lord. Every attempt is made to maintain integrity with the biblical text, and to avoid making contradictory statements, though there is much latitude for creative expression where the Holy Scriptures are silent.

Many of the main characters are predictably chosen, for the Gospel writers focus much of their writing on the last seven days of Jesus's earthly life and ministry. The characters that interact with Jesus are generally common to each Gospel writer.

Naturally we would expect to see and hear from Peter and John, two of Jesus's closest followers. And, according to the Bible, Mary Magdalene was nearby throughout the Passover preparations. Leaders like Caiaphas, Herod, and Pontius Pilate, are reported to have been intimately involved in the trials and crucifixion. The Centurion was a necessary part of the death squad, yet, as a consequence of God's grace, arrives at a point of spiritual conviction.

Nicodemus and Joseph of Arimathea removed Jesus's body from the cross and prepared it for burial. Jesus's body was placed in the tomb belonging to Joseph of Arimathea.

However, some personalities at the cross are more obscure as very little attention is given to them in the Gospels. Whether they were present at the cross and the days following is speculative, or sentimental. Perhaps Lazarus listened to Jesus's last words as he recalled his own miraculous resurrection. What did Barabbas feel as he watched another die in his place? What were Judas Iscariot's last thoughts before he took his own life? Did the arrogance of the Sadducee ameliorate the pathos of the cross?

Still others have been placed, by the writer, in the vicinity of the crucifixion the day after the cross, even though we have few clues as to their actual whereabouts at that time. Here we observe Elizabeth, the mother of John the Baptist. Did the cross of Christ open emotional wounds caused by her son's martyrdom?

Was the shepherd of the manger also an observer at the cross? Had he followed the progress of the baby in the manger, through adolescence, to the adult ministry of Jesus? Did the natural point of contact with Jesus as the Good Shepherd resonate with the shepherds on the hillside who heard the heavenly messengers?

Was the boy whose lunch fed five thousand noticed among the mourners present at Golgotha? To what degree had he adopted the teachings of the Master? Was he a follower and disciple or merely a one-time listener, among a multitude of others who came to Jesus for teaching and healing?

While we know that Simon of Cyrene walked to Golgotha, we know nothing of his home and family. He is accorded merely a sentence or two in each of the synoptic Gospels. Why was he in Jerusalem at Passover?

The magi brought gifts to the boy-king, worshiping him in a house. Did they retrace the route and return years later to assess his progress? Had they come to Jerusalem to acknowledge his Lordship and kneel before him in worship? Could they have intervened in the trials and crucifixion? If they stood at the cross would they comfort Mary? Did they identify with the spiritual conviction of the Centurion?

We are fascinated by the person of Jesus Christ. His life and ministry, culminating in his death and resurrection, are truly life changing. The Word of God allegedly reveals all we need individually to find salvation. Yet many mysterious truths remain. The characters enmeshed in Jesus's life must certainly have grappled with the enigmas embodied in the Savior's ministry.

Inquisitive minds or every age search for answers. As we observe several Biblical personalities we seek to understand both their questions and their answers. As well, attempts are made to discern their gifts, motivations, priorities, and perhaps their fears Throughout we wish to see their humanness with which we can identify, and where possible, their spiritual qualities, to which we may aspire.

This treatise is an attempt to live with and listen to New Testament men and women, seeing through their eyes the central figure—Jesus. Through the lives of the others, we hopefully will see the Messiah, as we *Behold the Man*.

Magi: The Worshiping Travelers

I was the first to see the light. It was in the sky, more precisely, in the stars. Then, excitedly, I reported my findings to my friends. The unheard of heavenly phenomenon spurred us, like the mournful mewling of an abandoned camel calf, to investigate its meaning. In our experience the omen was absolutely unique. What did it mean? Was this the sign our fathers, and their fathers had foretold? I will never forget the feeling of divine guidance as we viewed the sign in the sky, as though the great Daniel was speaking.

Many generations ago the ancient prophet Daniel predicted a wonderful happening would occur in his land. He did not specify the time, but revealed we should be watching for divine omens. Daniel's prophecies were passed down to succeeding generations and held dear by our ancestors. Elders and religious leaders among the Medes and Persians concurred with Daniel's insight.

Could we see fulfillments in our lifetime? According to our forefathers, he had a deep appreciation for his God, whom he called Yahweh, the covenant God of Israel. Daniel praised the God of heaven and said,

"Praise be to the name of God for
ever and ever;
wisdom and power are his.
He changes times and seasons;
he sets up kings and deposes
them.
He gives wisdom to the wise
and knowledge to the discerning.

He reveals deep and hidden things;
he knows what lies in darkness,
and light dwells with him.
I thank and praise you, O God of my
fathers:
You have given me wisdom and
power,
you have made known to me what
we asked of you,
you have made known to us the
dream of the king." (Daniel 2:20-23)

Daniel was able to discern the meaning of the imagery within King Nebuchadnezzar's dreams. When consulted, Daniel always gave credit to his God as the one who revealed the interpretations. Many of the Medes and Persians embraced Daniel's faith in the covenant God of Israel. Daniel promised that the long-awaited Messiah should come from Abraham's offspring. The prophesied Messiah was to be the Savior of the world. But when could the world expect this wonderful visitation?

Our history records Daniel's spiritual influence in Babylon. He was brought to our land almost six centuries ago at the pinnacle of Persian power. One triumphant military campaign saw the Hebrew exiles and the spoils of war carried to Babylon during the reign of King Nebuchadnezzar. Among the exiles was a youthful Daniel whose wisdom and administrative skills were legendary.

But we should not forget his great faith. Daniel and his circle of friends brought a spiritual awareness to our country unlike anything ever recorded in our past. We have read of the impact of his devout faith, both on his people and on ours. Many in my own family adopted his teachings, and longed for the Messiah's arrival. Daniel prophesied that the Messiah will be acclaimed as King of Kings and Lord of Lords.

Some of our historians revealed their personal biases when reporting an earlier return of certain exiles to Jerusalem following the conquest of Alexander of Macedon. Feelings of hostility surfaced as the writers complained about freeing the captives. After many generations in captivity, some Hebrew families were permitted to journey back to their homeland with their sacred vessels which were used in worship. Others patiently lugged tools that would be needed to rebuild the walls of the beloved City of Jerusalem. Our rulers tolerated the gradual return of the emigrants, but hoped the exodus would be temporary and slow to a trickle. Now, centuries later, we were following the trade routes and migrating to the Holy Land. We, however, were bound to make the return journey home.

Heavenly apparitions have always been seen as indications of divine involvement in our world. We questioned, "Could they be evil omens? Might they be heralding a coming war, pestilence or famine? Should we anticipate divine blessing? Was heaven speaking to us after many years of silence?"

We were already prepared, by faith in the prophecies, to receive the phenomenon of the divine oracle from Daniel's God. The star instigated our journey. It appeared unexpectedly.

I challenged my friends, "Let us go to the land of the Prophets to discern if this is the fullness of time foretold by Daniel and his successors." We wished to find the King of the Jews. I longed to see the land of the Messiah. We hungered to worship in the Temple with Daniel's people, and, dare we hope, to see the Messiah in person.

Throughout our preparations the sign in the skies hovered above, capturing our attention as a protective beacon. If anything, its brightness intensified as we set forth from our homeland. We prayed for its continued guidance as we risked our very lives on the extensive journey one thousand miles west.

Stark mountain passes and expansive deserts challenged our resolve. Stockpiles of supplies had to be amassed to sustain men and animals for the excursion. Limited provisioning could possibly be found in isolated outposts between established settlements, but there were no guarantees that our needs would be met along the way. Our caravan needed to be self-sufficient.

The star beckoned us onward like a bright fireball in the night sky. Our line of travel reflected its cross-sky trajectory. Its brilliance continued many weeks, accompanying us on our long journey west. Our admiration of the star deepened with each passing night. A growing familiarity and alliance compelled us forward on a common pilgrimage. Along the way we spoke to others in the oases and along caravan routes, dismayed to discover that they had no knowledge of our star. Still we followed, trusting its influence, leading us toward the place of our quest. The ancient prophecies, revealed through Daniel, told of a coming king whose birth was to be preceded by a sign in the sky. This promise became embodied in our star.

What was this heavenly sign? Our seers and scholars paused in speculation, but reached no definitive conclusions. Whatever it was, it appeared, according to our scientists, as a unique symbol unlike any other in history. Some of our sages suggested it might be a new star unknown to previous astrologers.

However, I believe it was a grouping of smaller stars in a rare conjunction of heavenly bodies. That these stars appeared in Pisces, the fishes, which our astrologers called the House of the Hebrews, was a most significant omen. We were thus motivated to continue to follow its westward leading.

Naturally, we gravitated toward the seat of government in the Land of the Hebrews as we searched for the king. Approaching Jerusalem, we observed the influx of a teeming mass of pilgrims coincidental with our arrival. Citizens of the Roman world reportedly gathered in the town of their birth, in obedience to the mandate of Governor Quirinius who sought to collect tax revenues from them.

Undulating lines of fellow travelers elbowed one another for early consideration and favorable treatment from the harried tax collectors. Government officials themselves complained of the lineups, lengthy working days, the bureaucratic bungling and general chaos, all the while dutifully collecting fines and taxes from the angry but confused populace. "Why should this privation be occurring, and why now?" the people wondered. "What do we get from the greedy Romans?" And, "When will we cast off the oppressive Roman yoke?"

The teeming city was in turmoil. Buildings housing the government tax men were overflowing with citizens irate in forced subjection to

Roman laws. Haggling over tax assessments was the order of the day. Tense arguments accompanied by diverse emotions and impolite charades of gestures punctuated the conflicts.

The streets were impossibly overcrowded, more heavily clogged with meandering visitors than the shopping days at *souks* or flea markets. Progress through the milling multitudes was agonizingly slow. Most of the people were as disoriented as were we, unable to offer clear directions to us in our quest to find the King of the Jews. No one could understand our interest in the star. As best we could, we described the star and the time of its first appearance in our country. Referring to a log book of our travels, we demonstrated how it had led us to the Holy City. Confused city officials expressed bewilderment at our story, for no heavenly sign had been seen in Jerusalem. They voiced deep appreciation for our attempts to communicate using their own language, but much seems to have been lost in the nuances of the translations. Interpreters with us fared no better. Scepticism surrounding the details of the star colored the visit, putting us on edge in the presence of angry questioners. It was strongly implied that we were strangers to the truth.

King Herod's courtiers directed us to certain religious leaders. They were no help. They were equally dumbfounded, swearing on oath that there were no heavenly signs. Herod himself heard of our quest and summoned us to a secret meeting.

We sidled up to the palace courtyard expecting a diplomatic welcome from Herod's family, or at least from his retinue of servants. Instead we were roughly hustled into the inner recesses of the royal residence where prying eyes and ears of the public were of no avail. Our gifts of courtesy were regarded with suspicion. Herod's officials aided by Roman military personnel interrogated us.

Initially they focused on our homeland, but a specific line of questions emerged showing great concern about the star. When did it appear? What precise date? Where and in which direction was it seen? Are there representatives present who could give attestation to the veracity of our story? When was the star last viewed? What meaning had we placed on the omen in the heavens? What was the origin of our alleged delusion about the birth of a rival King of the Jews?

I felt that this last question was most pressing on Herod. His accusing eyes pierced through his darkly clouded demeanor to capture my gaze. He stared unflinching, waiting for my response. I looked away uneasily, seeking an escape from the intimidating ordeal. None of us could satisfy Herod's examination for our own search was yet to be fulfilled.

We hurried from the palace with great trepidation. Later we realized our fears were warranted as the Almighty communicated with us in a dream, warning us to distance ourselves from Herod and his evil plans. In a subsequent fit of paranoia Herod systematically slaughtered all infants less than two years of age. Reportedly Herod and his advisors received our declaration of the star and calculated back to when it first appeared before us. What evil plans did he have as a consequence of the information? Regardless, we could not get away from that deranged man soon enough.

One in our company consulted the scrolls of the prophets in hopes of finding divine guidance. The Prophet Micah promised a ruler would arise from Bethlehem;

"But you, Bethlehem Ephrathah,
though you are small among the
clans of Judah,
out of you will come for me
one who will rule over Israel,
whose origins are from of old,
from ancient times.
Therefore Israel will be abandoned
until the time when she who is in
labor gives birth
and the rest of his brothers return
to join the Israelites.
He will stand and shepherd his flock
in the strength of the Lord,
in the majesty of the name of the

Lord his God.
And they will live securely, for then
his greatness
will reach to the ends of the earth.
And he will be their peace." (Micah 5:2-5)

Our search in Bethlehem proved fruitless. Yet stories abounded of an earlier heavenly visitation to a transient family in the town. Apparently they were taxpaying Roman citizens who had returned to the city of their birth. While in Bethlehem they welcomed a remarkable newborn baby into their home. Community leaders suggested that the family had relocated some miles away, maybe to the north.

We trudged to the hill country around Nazareth, but our search proved futile. The caravan crawled back to Bethlehem. Following a few scant clues pried from local citizenry, we eventually found the family and indeed the infant for whom we searched. In a tiny unprepossessing house nestled next to the shops on the edge of town we greeted the young couple and their infant son. With room enough only for a small family, the home felt overcrowded as representatives of our delegation quietly crept inside. The parents of the young infant welcomed us with unfeigned graciousness.

Instantly, we recognized a powerful presence, which contrasted with the humble surroundings. Surely we were in the presence of royalty. Royalty in every land in displayed amid trappings of jewelry and gold. Such would be expected at the crowning of a King. Thus, our gifts were certainly suitable for the occasion. While in our own land, we were reminded of gold as we considered the tales of Daniel's exile, and the golden spoils of war captured with the people. Protectively stashed away among our belongings were the carefully wrapped gifts of gold to be presented to the new King.

Next to the gold we laid another precious commodity. Frankincense comes from a gum derived from the balsamic tree or shrub. Late in the year the bark is incised and the resin obtained is collected and dried. Its nauseous taste is repellant to us but we respect its commercial value: for making incense. Its rarity makes frankincense costly as it is found neither in our land nor in the land of the Hebrews. Rather, it can only be obtained in trades with Arabia, Cush and Mizraim. Frankincense is used in the offerings of worship and an ingredient in holy ointment. What better gift could we possibly bring for the King?

Much like frankincense, myrrh is a rare dark red gum with a strong aroma, thought not as noxious to my nose. Another similarity is its origin, in Arabia and East Africa. We were able to acquire this precious luxury, an exquisite perfume and a special gift for the promised King, as we traveled along the trade routes in the lands east of the Holy City. Bartering for extravagant items is a way of life there. We offered our simple gifts—simple yet rare, since none of comparable quality could be found within this land. They were accepted gratefully, but with humble reluctance.

That night we received a holy vision, wherein we were warned to avoid the malevolent Herod. We obeyed this divine leading, and our homeward journey bypassed Jerusalem and the demented King. Following caravan routes directly east we moved past Petra, in Jordan, on the long road toward our distant home.

Our lives had been transformed by the pilgrimage. After we reached home the image and character of the boy-King continued to appear before us in recurring visions. For an entire generation I dreamed of the day we could return to worship the King.

At last we undertook to marshal our resources over several years until we could set our faces toward the west, re-commencing the difficult but rewarding journey. Our extensive entourage accompanied us along the overland trade routes.

This time we have better prepared for the arduous travel, and vast temperature swings through the desert areas that had little forage for the animals. We had several camel drivers to herd the beasts through the notorious *chamsins,* the sand storms that frequented the land of Daniel.

Our camels needed frequent reminders that they were to be servile, domesticated beasts of burden. Grooms fed and tended the beasts each day, ensuring the safety and protection of the caravan. Handlers were required to control cantankerous camels who bellow in rebellion against their heavy loads. Plus, there were more attendants in our company this time, as we were older and less robust to battle the elements. The extra assistants acted as a comforting presence should trouble from lurking evil opportunists arise along the way. Nefarious tribal chieftains often prowled the desert oases seeking instant wealth from unwary, ill-protected caravans. The meticulous records we had logged on our previous journey were often consulted to guide us around trouble spots.

The hot *chamsin* wind, burning by day but freezing at nightfall, continuously swept across the desert bearing dust and sand, stinging our unprotected flesh and nearly blinding us as we began the westward trek. Camels are accustomed to the wind-borne abuse, being created with compound eyelids to guard against sand storms, and great webbed feet to navigate in desert terrain. But man is more fragile.

Regardless of the privations, we steadfastly tightened our cloaks around us for protection, and soldiered on toward the Holy City, motivated to discover the status of the boy-King we had visited three decades earlier. We followed the well worn centuries-old trade routes for more than four full moons, all the while meandering westward toward the land of the Prophets. Purposely laid out to avoid areas of strenuous extremes, the route was nonetheless exceedingly difficult.

As we neared the King's land we were troubled by the unknown, not of the route but of the impending reception. We feared we would find Herod or one of his successors menacing the native people and visitors alike. Had the people accepted or rejected their new King? Was an age of peace upon us, or was civil disobedience the rule of the day?

Yesterday, we discovered that our fears were well founded. The populace was in a frenzy, bordering on chaos, as mob mentality ran riot in the city. Coarse shouts of derision thundered in the streets leading out from the city walls. Murderous threats were directed at three prisoners who were being brutalized by soldiers. "Crucify him" became a rallying cry for the rioting mob. We saw and heard hatred and evil beyond imagination. The appalling degradation sickened all of us.

Staggering along with the exhausted crowd we arrived at the Hill of the skull. Unspeakable cruelty was meted out against the severely beaten prisoners. Central to the scene of suffering was the one named Jesus of Nazareth. Printed on a placard and attached to the cross we read, "King of the Jews." Was this our King before whom we should bow? Had we traveled such a great distance to worship the King, only to arrive in time to witness his death and burial?

At the height of his suffering the executioners offered Jesus wine mixed with myrrh which acted as an anesthetic to ease the pain. The dying words of comfort from his bloodied lips were cherished by his grief-stricken mother.

"When Jesus saw his mother there and the disciple whom he loved standing nearby, he said to his mother, 'Dear woman, here is your son,' and to the disciple, 'Here is your mother.'" (John 19:26-27)

A gathering of disconsolate followers stood by helplessly, appearing to be deaf and mute to the horrors. In contrast, the majority in the vicious mob thirsted for his blood, mocking the crucified men. Jewish religious leaders and Roman executioners were complicit in the wicked deeds.

To us it seemed unbearably wrong. Through the hours of darkness we stood in reverence. Surely, our King was innocent? We watched as he was removed from the cross and prepared for burial. Aloes and myrrh were made into a mixture and wrapped around the body.

Daniel and the Prophets had foreseen this day. Some envisioned a triumphant Messiah. And others saw a suffering servant who would eventually rule in power. Could there arise from these people an atoning Messiah who would be acknowledged as King? Daniel spoke of the latter,

"Seventy years are decreed for your people and your holy city to finish transgression, to put an end to sin, to atone for wickedness, to bring in everlasting righteousness, to seal up vision and prophecy and to anoint the most holy." (Daniel 9:24)

Yesterday we observed Roman power subjugating the Messiah. Had we been here sooner, would it have made a difference? Could my wealth have purchased his release? We may have been able to offer a ransom, even a king's ransom to salvage the remnants of his kingdom.

It was prophesied that his kingdom was beyond this world. It was supposed to be a kingdom victorious over sin and death; a kingdom of peace. Daniel, who had received his inspiration from God, believed in the coming of a Messiah. The life and death of Jesus, the crucified one, had been foretold by the Prophets. We had seen him as the infant-King in his home in Nazareth, and as the heavenly King on the cross at Golgotha. Truly, we had found the One prophesied by Daniel.

The King was slain but his kingdom will live on. Wherever that spiritual kingdom exists, I wish to be part of it. I believe the Centurion revealed the truth, proclaiming Jesus to be the "Son of God." Yesterday they killed my King. Today and forevermore I will worship him.

A Shepherd: The Privileged Pilgrim

Where are God's heavenly messengers when we need them? Oh, if they had been here yesterday they could have exhibited divine power and overturned the sinfulness of wicked men. Our history shows angelic visitations occurring when God mystically intervenes in our world; when the supernatural communicates intimately with mortal men, validating the divine message. Why was yesterday the exception?

I am but a poor, rough shepherd. My training, however, fits well with my calling: raising sheep. Experience has taught me to value the tools of the trade. My pack, or bag made of goat skin, is a carryall in which, among other things, I place my sling for self-defense and for protection of the flock against wild animals. A small flute relieves the boredom of long nights and is a characteristically familiar sound to rally the flock. It also serves as an extension of my voice to calm the sheep. A cloak is included both for warmth and for bedding. A stick, used as a club and a shepherd's crook are indispensable for the protection of the animals.

My father was a shepherd, as was my grandfather, and I was taught at an early age the necessary skills. Shepherding is in our blood; it's a family tradition that has served us well. Most families have one or two sheep or goats, but for my family it was a way of life.

I am alone now. The rest of the family is gone. I miss the diligent care of my parents and the constant companionship of my brothers and sister. We worked together as a family to raise and tend the large flock of sheep along with a few goats. The resultant flocks are strong, healthy, and producing a modest living for me, but now all of the responsibility rests upon my shoulders. Each day I must find water for the herd, for though they may temporarily survive on sparse grasses, without water they will die. Night shelter is found in a sheep cote or in one of the many nearby caves.

My station in life is low, unappreciated by many. Many times I have strayed from the paths of righteousness. Brawling and cursing are natural to the brotherhood of shepherds. Often we have been banned from certain polite company due to our unappreciated life style. Priests would direct hostilities our way because we work on the Sabbath, designating us as lawbreakers. But there is no down time for a shepherd. Leaderless sheep do not survive.

Our critics make excuses citing our closeness to animals as the reason for their derision, relegating us to a kind of despised caste, asserting "they are different you know, since they are ceremonially unclean." Meanwhile they neglect to value our contributions which enhance their lives: milk to make yogurt and cheese, wool, skins and meat; and do not forget the essential sacrificial lambs. In the Torah God commanded, "This is what you are to offer on the altar each day: two lambs a year old. Offer one in the morning and the other at twilight. With the first lamb offer a tenth of an ephah of fine flour mixed with a quarter of a hin of oil from pressed olives, and a quarter of a hin of wine as a drink offering. Sacrifice the other lamb at twilight with the same grain offering and its drink offering as in the morning—a pleasing aroma, an offering made to the Lord by fire." (Exodus 29:38-40)

Priests today emulate our forefather Samuel when he, "Took a suckling lamb and offered it up as a whole burnt offering to the Lord. He cried out to the Lord on Israel's behalf, and the Lord answered him." (1 Samuel 7:9)

We have been defenseless against the cynicism of the disrespectful public, and the jealous bitterness of the religious leaders. Yet, I am a true believer in the Covenant God of Israel.

One night, I witnessed a miracle of the heavens. My eyes were accustomed only to visions of undulating grazing fields, with new born lambs nuzzling their mothers seeking food and warmth. Totally unprepared for the miracle of the ages, I strove to interpret the meaning of the divine revelation. Today, a generation later, I am filled with wonder; yes, and with fear, as I look back.

Even now I do not understand all I saw and heard on that unique night so long ago. My confused senses reported mixed messages, some difficult to believe. The night was cool and sweet as I watched the flock, protecting them from thieves and wolves. There have been thousands of such nights of tedious, routine labors. I ate simply, on fruit, unleavened bread and cheese. Sipping water kept me alert to my duties.

The night was well upon me but rest was unattainable, and a great uneasiness disturbed me. Something was not as it should be. A parched throat gave evidence of an abnormal feeling of apprehension. My mind was racing as though I was experiencing a premonition of the unknown. Something extraordinary commanded my attention, but as though numb, I was unable to understand it. An aura of awe covered the hillside. Strangely, there welled up within me an eerie paralysing fear. But, I scorned this fear and walked among the flock.

A different kind of stillness touched my senses. Change was moving over the hillside. It was the light. A strange sort of paleness gradually invaded the inky darkness. Brightness like that of a million oil lamps shone in the sky so that night became as day and day as brilliant shining silver. A great escalating glow made the faces of the others radient, brighter than reflections from the full moon. The soiled matted wool of the sheep began to glisten, as white as new fallen snow. We were surrounded by a magnificent light of unknown origin, out of which a glorious, God-like form emerged.

He appeared superior to us in every way. He was easily taller than any man, with a resonant voice, distinct as a mussein calling from a minaret. His beaming countenance encased piercing eyes, capturing my gaze. I listened intently for his words. What did his message mean? Caught between panic and promise I awaited further clarity.

Without warning came the wonderful angelic visitation. Other beings, first two, then four, eight; soon followed myriads filling the horizon, obscuring the stars. The numberless chorus raised their voices in musical anthems proclaiming glory to God. My feeble mind is still unable to encompass all that I experienced.

I feared for Bethlehem, my home town that it might be spared the searing flames of divine judgment for its sinfulness, which did happen to another city in former times. I hid my eyes in the deep grass of the hillside and trembled, captivated by fear. Vainly I sought to pray, but my tongue would not move, and my throat resembled burning sand of the desert.

From all directions came a great and solemn voice. It had a sound of gentleness, yet suffused with power and strength. I was instructed to rise, which I did in spite of my uncontrollable shaking. An authoritative voice clearly exhorted, "Fear not!" Under the circumstances I could not comply. My anxiety was out of control. The voice rolled in the hills and valleys. It bounded against rocks and crevices, and it echoed and re-echoed in my ears. I stood, cowering like a cold, lost sheep.

Though I searched for shelter from the foreboding presence, I turned to face the mountain of light. Great pain colored my senses. An angel of the Lord stood before me blocking out all peripheral vision. "I bring you good tidings of great joy!" He said it was for all people.

The good news focused on a baby, a new born baby, born in the City of David. That was my home, city of my birth. Then the messenger told us what to look for, and how we would recognize him. We should seek a stable wherein we would find a manger cradling a baby in strips of cloth. As mysteriously as they appeared they were suddenly gone. Silence descended over the hills.

Far off other shepherds stood as I, in silent awe, imprisoned by fear. On the distant horizon brown goat skin tents scattered among the barren hills heaved like the bellies of stricken cattle. Were others stirred by the divine revelation? Would this message impact all people, or a select few? Was the whole of creation affirming the glorious heavenly announcement of the Messiah's arrival?

The angel had spoken in words of gentle instruction that to the world on this day was born in Bethlehem, the City of David, a child who was the Savior, Christ the Lord. The instructions specified the child lay clothed in strips of cloth in a stable of the city. I recalled being taught by my father to watch for the arrival of the Messiah. He spoke of hope in every generation that the Messiah would come to free his people. Was this the fulfilling of Micah's prophecy as he envisioned;

"But you, Bethlehem Ephrathah
though you are small among the
clans of Judah,
out of you will come for me
one who will be ruler over Israel,
whose origins are from of old,
from ancient times.
Therefore Israel will be abandoned
until the time when she who is in
labor gives birth
and the rest of his brothers return
to join the Israelites.
He will stand and shepherd his flock
in the strength of the Lord
in the majesty of the name of the
Lord his God.
And they will live securely, for then
his greatness
will reach to the ends of the earth,
And he will be their peace." (Micah 5:2-5)

Bethlehem was not far. My brothers and I immediately journeyed to the city. We moved apprehensively toward the town. Guided by a supernatural presence, we found the infant exactly as the angel prophesied. In an animal's feeding trough within a stable I watched a young mother adoring her new born baby. Her husband protectively stood nearby, as I had often done when tending new born lambs.

"Can it be," I asked, "that in this stable a child was born tonight?" The anxious father affirmed the facts as we had been told. "May we look upon this child? For he is the Savior as our fathers have taught would come into the world."

The man was pleased but not surprised. We knelt and worshiped.

Never was there a child like this. These were poor people, but this was no ordinary birth. It was a miracle. This could only be the unfolding of the message from heaven, given on the hillside. God had come into our world, as foretold by the prophets. Holiness touched us, for from the baby came brilliance, not of light, nor of color, but of a substance unknown.

My limbs became weak. Tears and fears welled up within me. Once more I wept, for I had witnessed the wonder of the ages. The Messiah had come!

We worshiped him there. We became special eyewitnesses to heaven's supernatural revelation. Shepherds had never before been so privileged. Afterward we went out into the night in awe, fear and wonderment. God's ancient promise had been kept. Christ the Savior was born!

In subsequent and intervening years his followers asserted, "He grew in stature and favour with God and man." His incomparable wisdom astounded the sages and teachers of Israel. When he became an adult a select group of spiritual zealots acknowledged him as the "Lamb of God who takes away the sin of the world." The one in the manger was recognized as the Messiah.

The man called Jesus referred to himself as, "The Good Shepherd." He identified with us. "The sheep listen to his voice," he said. "He calls his own sheep by name and leads them out." He understood the heart and soul of a shepherd. He enthusiastically continued, reassuring his followers, "I am the good shepherd. The good shepherd lays down his life for the sheep. I know my sheep and my sheep know me—just as the father knows me and I know the father—and I lay down my life for the sheep. I have other sheep that are not of this sheep pen. I must bring them also. They too will listen to my voice, and there will be one flock and one shepherd. The reason my father loves me is that I lay down my life—only to take it up again." (John 10: 4, 11, 14)

His wonderful words were meaningless to those who disregarded the invaluable role of shepherds. They were were fulfilling and prophetic. He was one of us, my Shepherd-King.

I could not hear his weakened voice as he crumbled in defeat yesterday at the cross? The quietness of Bethlehem's stable contrasted to the harsh cries amid Golgotha's gory execution. The brutal, sadistic soldiers approached their assignments like barbarians thirsty for blood, vying for approval from their superiors. Compassion for another's suffering was a foreign concept, beyond their experience, and viewed as a betrayal of their training. Animals are spared such torture and could not survive the inhumane brutality. Sacrificial lambs are accorded greater deference.

Yesterday, emotions raged out of control among the stunned observers. Of the attending women, most were close relatives or devout followers. Naturally they were overcome by the traumatic scene. Many were in various stages of shock. They stood as if turned to stone. It is not that they did not move, they could not move. They were even incapable of fleeing from the grotesque scene.

The publicly impartial politicians were pretending to be detached from the execution. Some were simply reticent, while a few were embarrassed by complicity in the travesty. With their masks of neutrality stripped away many joined the Good Shepherd's enemies and hurled wicked epithets in his direction.

Few devout believers, other than John, could stomach the grotesque horror. It was too much. I had to turn away. Even the heavenly messengers were silent, withholding their power, neglecting to intervene in heaven's passion play.

What were the expectations of the mob? What hopes were held by the crucified one's family? What beliefs were espoused by his followers in his final hours? Did any of them revere his teachings? Did the priests consult the Torah or the Prophets for divine inspiration or prophetic insight?

A good shepherd protects the flock. The Good Shepherd gave his life for his sheep. Why did the others miss the truth? I believe heaven has profoundly spoken again.

Elizabeth: The Heartbroken Mother

What's a mother to do? I tried to do my best. They cannot criticize my efforts or my motives. I relished being a mother, John's mother. He needed me amid the triumphs and the traumas. When John was arrested, and the police charged him with attempting to incite a riot, and seeking to overthrow the government, I was inconsolable. How could there ever be justification for breaking the law? When he was arraigned my maternal care and pride were torn from me. What would my family think? How would the fellowship of followers react? Disbelief, sadness and grief enveloped my world.

The evil atmosphere of a prison was foreign to me. I was out of my element. This was the son I raised. He was our joy and delight. He had been conceived in love, and raised responsibly. John was cared for with diligent concern, educated, dreamed about and upheld daily in prayer. He was all we could hope or ask for.

The jailers were unsympathetic. Immoderate protesters and rebels like John were daily phenomena they had seen too often. I soon abhorred what some dismiss as alternate lifestyles.

Where did I go wrong? How did I fail? The guards had no empathy for my tears. What happened to my son? He appeared as an angry young man with long unkempt, filthy hair. Around his waist was a leather belt and he wore a jacket made of animal skins. He apparently had been living on the streets as a homeless man for quite some time. His diet of insects and the like was in keeping with his appearance. John refused to eat regular food. He said he preferred a natural diet, whatever that means. He certainly did not acquire his bizarre tastes from our table at home.

Maybe the rumors were right, as for many months he had acted so oddly. At best he was strange, and perhaps even mentally imbalanced. His bizarre behavior was the talk of the town: his eccentricities more galling than cute. Similar aberrations do not run in our families. I thought a good lawyer could make a difference, but it was merely a waste of time and money. John was taught to always respect authorities. When had he developed such arrogance and rebelliousness? He was courteous and respectful in our home, and his behavior toward his relatives was a model of decorum. He had to be dragged out of court during his own hearing for calling the judge an immoral man. Before that episode I believed John was a man of some wisdom. However, he chose to attack the one whose word determined whether he would live or die. Can you believe it?

We tried to bring him up right. My husband Zacharias prayed with John every day. We were faithful in attendance at worship and in the many youth activities. I was a stay-at-home mother, never neglecting my son's needs. We gave John our constant attention, with quality time, doing this joyfully. Of course we were older than most parents, but age of childbearing was out of our control. We dedicated him to God when he was a baby and his whole life was relinquished to the guidance of God's good hand. Every day I could see him serving the Lord in some future capacity. I wanted his life to be an offering to God, so then I was puzzled. Why did God allow bad things to happen?

John was a beautiful baby. His chubby face and sparkling eyes brightened any room. Childhood was a time of contented learning and steady growth. My strong, healthy, handsome son loved the outdoors. He seemed interested in every possible pursuit. We made sure he had the best education, and did not neglect his biblical training. Zacharias and I saw to it that John knew the Torah and the Prophets. As a family we read the Holy Scriptures in our home. Attendance at worship was both a joy and a lifestyle. We were pleased to hear John's frequent questions about God. He often inquired why people acted the way they did, especially people in the fellowship.

When did he change? I did not see it coming. He actually embarrassed us in front of the congregational leaders, by his attitude. His aberrant behavior was a thorn in my side for years but he could not see it. He actually thought he was doing God's will. I told Zacharias it was impossible to do God's will while looking like a vagrant. Alienating the entire religious community did not help either. The family regarded him as the black sheep of the flock. With his talents and education John could have been a fine leader among God's people, who would have truly listened to him. Sadly, he did everything his own way, living from hand-outs and acquiring a police record.

Every mother feels elated after the birth of her child. But, for Zacharias and me the feeling was particularly exquisite. John was a divine answer to prayer. We had been childless for 25 years and our hope of becoming parents was gone. So, you can see why we considered John a gift from God. All I ever wanted was to be a wife and mother. Zacharias himself was an answer to my prayers. He is a fine man, devoted to God, to me and our son. Our family was respected in the community. In the early years I was constantly visiting doctors. Day after day we prayed and cried pleading with God for a child. Specifically we longed for a son. Following interminable tests the doctors announced I was in perfect health, so physically I should be able to bear children.

"Barren" is such a cruel word. It made me resent God, for had I not prayed? Why did God not hear? The doors of heaven were incomprehensibly slammed in my face.

Zacharias was busy at work, preparing Torah studies, meeting the religious leaders, directing committees, administering budgets, and performing the others tasks necessary to keep the body of believers going. It was different for me. I had more time to think and to pray. My life was so lonely. Whenever friends or relatives got together the conversation gravitated to talk of children. They were never cognizant of my pain. Gradually I distanced myself from their gatherings. I formulated excuses saying I was busy or not feeling well. I was being truthful. I felt horrible, like a cursed woman, and blight on society, shunned by my heavenly father.

Had I lived in Hannah's era I may have had a ready ear and an understanding heart. Like her I also wished for a son who could be used by God. Her long awaited son grew up to become a godly priest.

Hannah's prayer began:
> "My heart rejoices in the Lord;
> in the Lord my horn is lifted
> high.
> My mouth boasts over my enemies,
> for I delight in your deliverance.
> There is no one holy like the Lord;
> there is no one besides you;
> there is no Rock like our God." (1 Samuel 2:1-2)

I had prayed. Where was my deliverance? My God was definitely not Rock-like. Were her prayers more effective than mine? Had I failed God?
> "The Lord brings death and makes
> alive;
> he brings down to the grave and
> raises up.
> The Lord sends poverty and wealth;
> he humbles and he exalts.
> He raises the poor from the dust
> and lifts the needy from the ash
> heap;
> he seats them with princes
> and has them inherit a throne of
> honor.
> For the foundations of the earth are
> the Lord's;
> upon them he has set the world.
> He will guard the feet of his saints,
> but the wicked will be silenced in
> darkness." (1 Samuel 2: 6-9)

I longed for a son to follow in his father's footsteps. Why had God refused to heed my pleadings? Zacharias and I had followed the Torah teachings, so why had God not guarded the feet of his saints? The fellowship of believers needed a leader and unifying force; a light in the darkness. A son could be the answer to many prayers.

In those days we seldom talked. In fact, Zacharias traced his speech problems to an encounter with a heavenly messenger within the Holy Place while offering incense. Unable to speak, he resorted instead to communicating using a writing tablet. Think of the stress that put on our relationship. My husband kept the specific details to himself for several weeks.

Then one marvelous day, with no forewarning, my prayers were answered even as questions multiplied. Was this a divine hoax? Did the doctor make a mistake? Me, pregnant? How should it be announced? What should I tell people? Am I ready for this? What about my physical health and proper nourishment? What will people think? How is this miracle possible for a woman of my age?

The next weeks flew by as I prepared for the new arrival. I learned why God ordinarily ordained pregnancy for younger women. Still, I never complained of my aching old bones nor of the exhaustion I felt, as I basked in the euphoria of answered prayer. I felt like a real woman for the first time in years. Daily I was praising God among his covenanting people.

I was so into myself I failed to understand my husband's strange behavior. Upon questioning he related a story about a visitation from an angel. Apparently Gabriel announced that he was to become the father of the precursor of the Messiah.

Zacharias was incredulous. Exuberantly, I exclaimed I was indeed pregnant. He was shocked. As he was still unable to verbalize, our one sided conversation took all afternoon. I directed his attention to God's goodness and faithfulness, and his continual blessings. Imagine me instructing a man of God, and after the struggles I had had with unanswered prayer. If God could bring about a miracle in my body he could certainly correct a mute voice.

Maybe it was my husband's age—he is getting on in years—or a long hidden physical defect. He did get over it, miraculously, at the dedication of our baby where he persisted with his unusual habit of communication. He believed he was called by God to serve as a priest, and had many years of experience leading Temple ceremonies. Yet, that day was the most joy-filled occasion in our memory. After announcing our son's name Zacharias celebrated a new son, and a new tongue ever ready to shout praises to God.

John had a brief but successful career leading God's people. Dozens of followers adhered to his scholastic coattails and revered his spiritual guidance. He spoke as though inspired by the Spirit of God. He elevated the ancient ritual washing of purification, adopting the Greek vernacular "baptism." John proclaimed it as a life changing experience, available to all believers, stressing that in former times ritual cleansing was restricted to the priests. John's popularity soared along with his appeal, which produced a revival in the community.

He used unheard of language and spiritual terms connoting penitence. Unfortunately, when he moved outside of our traditional fellowship of believers to teach his doctrines, John attracted more enemies than disciples. First it was the religious leaders. Then the civic authorities came after him.

Mary, my cousin, had a son about six months after John was born. We used to visit one another during our pregnancies. She had many questions, thinking that with my age would come experience and wisdom. She was still in her teens. Her condition triggered oppressive anxieties. But, talk about a miracle! Her life was completely fulfilled. After her son was born we lost touch. Her whole family, Mary, Her husband and her son moved away, and relocated to another city upon their return.

Later, I heard that Mary was having trouble with her son. It shocked me to hear it. He was always so polite to my friends, though Zacharias said he could be rather curt with some of the religious leaders. He tended to stay around home to work with his father, as part of the family business. Mary said lately he worked less at home and spent more time traveling. He hung out with less refined friends. A rough crowd followed his teachings, many of them fishermen from the docks who were easily inflamed by religious fanatics or political zealots. For a while he had a large following of supporters, until something happened that split them up, and most just dropped out.

John refused to elaborate on a mysterious meeting he had with

Mary's son. He intimated I should revere Jesus more than any other person. He raved incessantly about the promised Messiah. Initially I was confused, for even though many false prophets have littered the pages of our history, few survived long enough to establish an enduring following. Was Jesus another in the long line of pretenders?

I sought answers as I perused Zacharias's scrolls of the Torah and the Prophets. I discovered that Isaiah's prophecies concerning the Messiah corroborated John's passionate pleadings and the angel's announcement to Zacharias. Not only did Mary have a miraculous pregnancy as Isaiah foretold, but the life and ministry of Jesus gave irrefutable evidence of his heavenly identity. John's once audacious declarations now seemed entirely credible: Jesus was the Messiah!

The monster Herod, had orchestrated his death, just as he did John's. John was defenseless, vulnerable and innocent. What could I do? Still, the guilt eats away at my self-esteem. If I was too old to be a proper mother why did God allow the pregnancy?

We did our best. We gave sacrificially. I prayed earnestly. I know I did not cope well with John's rebellion. Zacharias and I were victimized. I understand Mary's pain. And yesterday my grieving was brought back with brutal force at the murder of her son. Mary will need my support, solace and care. She too is a victim.

I did not think it would go that far for either my John or for Mary's boy. It is almost more than a mother can bear. Mary said, "He was always God's son, only loaned to me for a time."

How could she be so certain? Is that how she feels today? I wish I could comfort her broken heart.

Nicodemus: The Inquisitive Student

I did not know him very well, or very long; hardly a year. Yet, I perceived Jesus to be an authentic visionary, capable of startling penetration and insight. He had such depth of understanding as to be God-like. Had he lived longer there is no telling what heights he may have reached.

I am but one voice on the Council, known formally as the Sanhedrin. We are a select court of scribes, priests, and rabbis. We are venerated as much for our advanced age as for knowledge of court procedures.

The high priest announced at our Council meeting that he did not trust the Galileans. That revelation hardly qualified as news. He said he was afraid these trouble-making renegades, as he called them, might try to steal the body from the tomb. "Why on earth would they do that?" I blurted.

From others arose a murmur of puzzlement. The high priest jumped in, "You recall the impostor saying what would happen after he spent three days in the grave. What is to stop his followers from stealing the body and spiriting it away, then telling everyone he has risen? Even you, Nicodemus must see that the last fraud would be worse than the first."

"Risen from the grave?" I asked. "You mean they will report his disappearance and thus claim he came back to life? That is preposterous. Who would believe them?"

As usual Caiaphas the High Priest, who presided later at the night trials of Jesus, exploited the judicial system to his own benefit. He made it appear as if his way was the only way, which meant asking

Pilate to assign Roman soldiers to guard the tomb. After some posturing and sneering Pilate gave his permission. By the afternoon a Centurion's tent was erected 25 meters away from the entrance to the tomb. Guards were appointed to alternate watches. The two on duty were required to keep the doorway in sight at all times.

The high priest inveigled his way into the action, taking everyone by surprise. Across the center of the stone blocking the entrance he ordered a taut cord to be strung as a kind of seal. With dabs of mortar he fastened the two ends of the cord to the tomb wall. As his command was being carried out the soldiers openly grumbled, fearing they were not trusted. They were right. The seal was the high priest's subtle way of informing them that they also were under scrutiny. There was to be no bribery or professional lapses to reflect back to Caiaphas.

I shivered in sympathy last evening as I thought of Jesus lying in that dank chamber. The heavily guarded tomb stimulated remorse, not just for his interment but for my earlier disinterest. I reminisced, reviewing my timid questions during our first encounter.

It was just over a year ago. Still it galls me to recall the surreptitious late night meeting. Afraid of what my colleagues might say behind my back if they were aware of my visit, I sneaked into the house under cover of darkness. I furtively crept along like a convict on the run, or a pathetic fugitive fleeing from the authorities.

You can understand my reluctance to be discovered. To take a stand in support of an unorthodox Rabbi is to commit vocational suicide. There can be mistakes made by a teacher in my position. My decisions are constantly open to questions; every action is scrutinized, making me vulnerable. Thus it was necessary to meet the Rabbi in private.

Privacy was my ally; there was no need to enrage my fellow Councillors. The Master welcomed me, expressing deep concerns for our nation's and my own future, and sharing as with a close confidant.

He honored me in our conversation by acknowledging the desperate earnestness that drove me to him. I was pleased when he chose to ignore my aristocratic wealth and bearing, which contrasted with his poverty-stricken background. He respected my educational status when he confessed, "You are the teacher of Israel," and "ruler of the Jews."

My attempts to hide my deepest feelings failed miserably. He saw right through me, whereas the Sanhedrin, the ruling body of Judaism, was deceived by my outward conformity and compliance. My intelligence, achievements and refined culture, admired by colleagues, were considered as excess baggage by the insightful Rabbi.

What was I doing there? Since I was the official religious teacher of the righteous community he should have sought an audience with me. I entered his presence by night not seeking concealment so much as privacy. I needed no rivals competing for his attention. I tried to praise him through courtesies, crediting him with divine power. After all, he was a favored Galilean teacher.

Seeking truth, I requested an explanation of the Master's unique doctrines and power. He replied with a list of conditions for spiritual understanding. He emphasized that truth was not found by mental reasoning but by a radical reconstruction of the entire personality. Perplexed, I confessed wonder at that point. How could these things be?

"Born again," he announced. "Everyone must be born again." Thinking I was well informed on the concept, he proceeded to teach in an atmosphere of awe and wonder. Apparently the need to be born again was a cardinal doctrine of the Rabbi. He went on to tell me how I could become acceptable in the eyes of God. Since we are unable to save ourselves we require God's supernatural work in our lives.

While my attention was piqued, I remained shocked and totally confused. The discussion was at odds with the body of orthodox teaching codified in our rabbinical parchments. The Master pressed on with a series of questions. I tried to please him with answers that I hope he expected, but I fear I failed.

Then I speculated that he might foretell when God would act and restore the kingdom to Israel. But he disappointed me. He quickly detoured around that controversy, reiterating his favorite subject of my prospective new birth.

Both of us were sitting there in the dark, a table between us, on which was resting a dimly flickering oil lamp. As the flickering intensified he appropriately introduced the subject of the wind, implying a certain spiritual significance. He said the unsearchable ways of the Spirit were exemplified by the wind. It always blows where it will, but you cannot tell where it comes from or where it goes. When I asked him to further explain this enigma he countered, "Are you the teacher in Israel, Nicodemus, and you do not understand?" My eyes darted away from his penetrating, all-knowing gaze. I was grateful for the darkness that hid my blushing face.

I never questioned the need to be born again but I definitely doubted the possibility. How can we be changed so completely as to be born again? The Rabbi responded according to God's revelation to the Prophet Ezekiel:

"Prophesy to these bones and say to them, 'Dry bones, hear the word of the Lord! This is what the Sovereign Lord says to these bones: I will make breath enter you, and you will come to life. I will attach tendons to you and make flesh come upon you and cover you with skin; I will put breath in you, and you will come to life. Then you will know that I am the Lord.' " (Ezekiel 37:4-6)

Life is to be renewed by the breath of God's spirit in response to prayer. Dead bones are enlivened with new flesh. God, through Ezekiel, clearly applied these truths to my people:

"Son of man, these bones are the whole house of Israel. They say, 'Our bones are dried up and our hope is gone; we are cut off.' Therefore prophesy and say to them: 'This is what the Sovereign Lord says: O my people, I am going to open your graves and bring you up from them; I will bring you back to the land of Israel. Then you, my people, will know that I am the Lord, when I open your graves and bring you up from them.'" (Ezekiel 37:11-13)

What did it mean to be born again? Jesus said it is the work God does to enliven the spirit of man so he can communicate with God. It is God's ministry of restoration in our lives. The Rabbi challenged me to discover these truths.

Bewildered, I pressed him for clarity. "Are you certain?" How can a person be reordered, renewed, and reborn? Patiently he continued the lesson, answering, "By obedience, surrender and praise."

I staggered away from our conversation unable to come to grips with the implications. I was confused as I crept away to my home. I was unable to sleep, lying awake while seeing in memory his calm face with direct eyes that seemed to penetrate my soul.

Surprisingly, the truths came back to me last week at the palm procession. When the Pharisees, my fellow religious leaders, publicly protested about the chaotic processional I supported their complaints. Well, at least I refused to join in the condemnation of the Rabbi's followers. I admit, to my embarrassment however, no "Hosannas" crossed my lips.

My mind cannot erase the memory of the awful, heartbreaking appearance of his face yesterday at the cross. Was this the one I had chosen to believe? The trials and beatings had weakened him to the point of exhaustion. His visage, formerly gentle and compassionate, had been painfully rearranged by the torturous countdown to the cross. At Golgotha death came quickly.

Throughout the spectacle he struggled to breathe, repeatedly shifting his weight from his hands to his feet and back again. Every time he slumped down and hung by his arms the burden of his body weight prevented his lungs from properly filling. At last, gasping for air, he could neither raise himself nor catch his breath. In spite of the incredible horror of the cross, it is eerie to think that his death was, in the end, a matter of suffocation. There was no need for the soldiers to break his legs.

He had been hanging there, dead, just a few moments when Joseph arrived back from town. He showed a writ with the Governor's signature granting permission to take the body. He brought along the linen. It was the beginning of the Sabbath. Time was too short to finish the cleansing, the anointing, and the rest of the burial processes, so the linen cloth served as a temporary shroud. It would have to suffice until the Sabbath passed and the women could come to properly complete the embalming.

The battered, disfigured body was removed from the cross by the soldier-executioners. A task summoning utmost care was in this case eschewed by the military. Familiarity with death offered no qualification for actually dealing with burial procedures. Finally his body was lowered from the cross. Two of my servants hoisted the corpse, lifting it by the head and feet.

Joseph and I led the way, down the slope descending from the north side of the hill. The mute, steady gaze of onlookers focused on the lifeless remains of the Rabbi. Most saw where we were headed—to the tomb, hewn out of soft limestone and tunneled into a large outcropping at the foot of Golgotha hill. When we reached the vestibule my two men handled the body like a rare treasure and positioned it on a strip of matting. Two huge jars of spices were waiting nearby. I had sent ahead this mixture of myrrh and aloes suspended in olive oil.

Inside, the yellowish glare of a small torch held by one of the servants, cast our shadows grotesquely on the dank, dingy walls. We spread a thin layer of the spice mixture along the top of the stone bench. Half of a long linen cloth was neatly stretched atop the bench, leaving the other half rolled up at the head. With deliberate care we eased the body lengthwise on the linen.

We lifted and crossed the wrists, tied them together with short strips of linen, and then arranged them restfully on his stomach. Joseph bound his bearded jaws with another strip of cloth, passing it under the chin and over the top of his head. The usual coins were laid on the eyes. We had to borrow some from my servant. He had only some poorly stamped ones turned out by Pilate's mint, which was ironic, but fitting. Fragrant perfume from the spices permeated the sepulcher, masking the stench of death.

Out of my devotion to him I ministered to his broken body. The last tortured days of his life were mercifully past. I decided he would have at his death the ceremonial honor denied him in life.

Finished for the day, Joseph and I stood in respectful silence, surveying the scene of interment. It was all so wrong. His expressive hands were unmoving, stiff and paralysed. His agile tongue was silenced. His limbs of miraculous healing were unbending and lifeless.

We emerged as dusk enveloped the garden. The servants waited to see the stone set in place, eyeing the soldiers with suspicion. We had all seen to many abuses of power to trust this Roman guard.

The great stone rubbed and scrapped along the tomb wall, and within the canted groove in the ground. It gave off a loud rumbling, rattling sound as if it were groaning and gasping. I shuddered, as the eerie noise grated on my ears. My limbs quivered as a pall swept over the grave site.

After Sabbath I will finish the burial. It is hard to believe it is over. He said "It is finished." Did he intend us to perceive the grave as finality? Wait! The Rabbi taught the essential truth: we must be born again. He adamantly proclaimed those who are born again have eternal life, according to the Holy Scriptures:

"I will put my Spirit in you and you will live, and I will settle you in your own land. Then you will know that I the Lord have spoken, and I have done it, declares the Lord." (Ezekiel 37: 14)

I tried to hide and could not. When asked to defend him I would not. My mortal life will be meaningless if I continue to negate his teachings. As the teacher of Israel I will henceforth reveal the testimony of one who has been born again.

A Boy with a Huge Lunch: The Generous Contributor

I followed along eagerly anticipating his captivating teaching, and hoped to see spectacular wonders of healing. I was not disappointed. Like the others who tagged along, I was not ready to let go, hanging onto every word and wishing the day would never end.

The crowd swelled in numbers as we meandered along the seashore and pathways bordering the village of Tiberias. They intended to intersect the path of the boat when it landed on the north shore of the Sea of Galilee. Jesus and his disciples were visible on board. The boat was headed to a part of the lake that was well known to the people since a nearby hillside was the site of Jesus's earlier teaching.

Within the expectant crowd ashore were Jesus's friends and devout followers. Some of the crowd ran ahead. Others walked briskly, or limped painfully. The entire assembly exhibited an urgent need to meet the Master. Some issued painful pleas imploring the Master's attention. In the throng were those with infirm family members in tow, seeking divine intervention, and begging for the Lord's healing touch. So great were their needs that the multitude was committed to staying all day and long into the evening.

I spied a few critics and enemies of the Master hidden within the masses, waiting to trap him, and subsequently to charge him with heresy. Of course he was charged, but on technicalities of the ceremonial law, and he was always found sinless.

It had been a long day. The sun was low on the horizon as we settled on the hillside. Jesus's power was the story on everyone's lips. Nothing and no one could match his reputation. People tried to recall if other rabbis or teachers had such impact in past history, but none could be found.

It seems Jesus's fame was well deserved. His popularity surpassed that of the rabbis and priests, and even of the politicians. I never tired of his spiritual teaching. On the contrary, I hungered for more divine truths. His preaching was applicable to my life. No one had ever spoken spiritual truths as he did. Truly, this one was from God.

The extreme heat of the day had a dreadful effect on everyone, especially on the lame and infirm. Their strength was sapped. I found that shallow breathing was necessary in the muggy air.

Perhaps out of compassion for the ill, the teacher's close friends wished to send the crowd away to fend for themselves. I heard Philip say that they could not possibly supply an adequate amount of food. But wouldn't you know it, Jesus had a more Godly response, using this opportunity to test his disciples' faith. Being aware of his inability to finance an adequate supply of food, Philip wished the crowd would be dispersed to find their meals. "Eight month's wages would not buy enough bread for each one to have a bite," he said.

I thought of the few tiny fish in my uneaten lunch but considered them insignificant in the face of such great need. The small Tilapia fish have large silvery-pink scales covering delicate, juicy white flesh. Barely a third of a meter in length, they are somewhat distended with a girth of half their length. Customers flock to the market to buy the daily catch. The Sea of Galilee is shallow, never greater than fifty meters in depth where these fish thrive. They hover in the shallow coves to feed before moving away to slightly deeper waters.

As a boy I learned to fish using a hand-cast net thrown from shore. As I became more adept I gained notoriety and friends among the fishermen. Hanging around the docks afforded opportunities to hop on board boats moving away from shore for more productive fishing spots. My labor was bartered in exchange for a portion of the catch.

Fish spoil rapidly in the heat and humidity of Tiberias unless treated carefully and promptly. If the catch was to be consumed within a few days the fish were temporarily stored in salt water. Longer storage required proper preservation on salt. Family traditions prevailed as my parents led me in curing the fish. My father taught me the proper methods of preserving fish, which he learned from his parents. Each time he insisted there was only one way to save the catch and then demonstrated his method.

He was a stickler for details. His deep voice boomed with authority to emphasize the importance the task. My father's instructions were repeated so often I memorized the entire process:

The fish are placed and carried in a bucket. One by one they are washed in clean water. The two small fins behind the gills are removed so as to stimulate the work of salt in preserving the fish. Cover the bottom of a large clay jar or cask with a layer of coarse sea salt. Atop the salt a layer of fish is placed. Continue alternating salt and fish until the container is full, with a final layer of salt on top. Leave in the jar 6 to 8 weeks, until the curing is complete, and the fish are dried, inspecting and adding salt periodically if necessary. After the fish are thoroughly preserved the salt is washed away, the fish cleaned with heads and tails removed and the bones discarded by removing the backbone. Finally, rinse the fish before placing in clean clay jars for storage.

My mother always cheerfully helped me salt the fish. Her eyes sparkled whenever I demonstrated a knack for the essential skill of preserving fresh fish. It was a staple at the family table complemented by fresh bread which was baked daily. As a young boy I was unappreciative of those pleasures. Later, I realized how richly blessed I was in my family home. In the days of my youth I recall my mother cooking the occasional catch over an open fire. Any surplus was salted and preserved for future feasts.

The morning of the miracle lunch I reached into the precious store of preserved fish and selected two for my lunch to go with five freshly baked unleavened rolls of Matzot. Late in the afternoon the crowd began to noticeably tire, as did the Master. I heard the fishermen, his followers, mention he was exhausted from a grueling schedule; also he was grieving over the death of his cousin, John the Baptizer, who was murdered by Herod.

The milling mob was caught in a quandary, wishing to hear more from the Teacher, yet faint from the intense, humid heat rising from the nearby lake.

A few disgruntled stragglers, ruled by their stomachs, slipped away from the gathering to return to their kitchens and homes. Unfortunately for them they missed seeing the awesome power of Jesus's miraculous provision. The Master and his close friends felt sorry for the famished listeners. Some disciples offered personal opinions concerning the dilemma, but admitted they had no solutions.

Moments before, I observed Andrew as he sought food offerings from the assembled followers. When he approached me he had a momentary shock of recognition, remembering our personal encounters at the fishing docks. Soon all of the disciples moved away from the Master, pushed through the crowd and asked if anyone had food to spare. None was found.

Andrew and Peter, whom I knew from the fishing fleet, approached me with the same request. They saw the skimpy scraps of food—a few dried fish I had caught in the Lake, along with some unleavened bread my mother had baked. The small lunch was carried in a pack slung around my neck.

Andrew watched me unwrap the prized morsels. Wishing I had eaten earlier, and knowing the tedious labor involved in preserving fish and baking rolls, I nevertheless could not refuse them and handed over my meager lunch to Andrew, who passed it on to Jesus. The Lord received it as a precious gift.

He caught my eye, holding me in his focus. How did he know it was my lunch, with fish I had caught and painstakingly preserved? While blessing the small lunch in prayer, not only did he thank me, he thanked God for my simple lunch. He broke the fish and bread into small pieces.

Then he gave portions to the disciples who distributed it to the crowd which had been seated in groups. There must have been thousands of them! And we were all astounded that there was more than enough for all of us to eat our fill. There were even many basketfuls left over after all were satisfied. Where had it all come from? We were amazed by the Master's miraculous touch.

After we had eaten, he continued to teach about faith, discipleship, and the kingdom of God. Many of the sick were made whole. That day I too became one of his followers.

The Master taught with authority in contrast to the religious leaders. I have attended Torah teachings all my life even though the lessons were usually boringly similar. Often my thoughts were on other things, and more personal, stimulating pursuits. The rabbis simply rehashed the old traditional stories and did so with waning enthusiasm and little insight. Rabbinic prayers, though overtly pious, seemed to me, to be wooden and out of touch. Not so the Master-Teacher. He had a way of presenting the truths of the Torah so that listeners were inspired to follow his teachings.

His prayers sounded like personal communication with the Almighty. Jesus subsequently taught his disciples a model prayer:
"Our Father in heaven,
hallowed be your name,
your kingdom come,
your will be done
on earth as it is in heaven.
Give us today our daily bread.
Forgive us our debts,
as we also have forgiven our
debtors.
And lead us not into temptation,
but deliver us from the evil one,
for yours is the kingdom
and the power and the glory
forever. Amen." (Matthew 6:9-13)

I memorized his prayer, repeating it several times each day. His disciples did likewise. The scribes, though publicly critical, were I believe, privately respectful, perhaps envious of the Teacher's obvious talents and deep spirituality, and of course of his faithful following.

Jesus healed with power unlike the physicians. Many of the sick were healed in an instant, in contrast to the months and years of lengthy therapies given out by the village doctors. Often, customary medical practices brought little comfort or cure, but Jesus really healed the sick! At his gentle touch the blind could see, or the deaf could hear, or the lame were made to walk; conditions beyond the abilities of the doctors.

Recently, when visiting in Bethany Jesus met with his dear friends Mary and Martha. They were mourning the death of their brother Lazarus. Their grieving intensified when they saw Jesus because they felt he had let them down by not coming sooner. Lazarus had been ill for many months and beyond hope according to the doctors. Jesus went right to the cemetery and stopped beside the grave. He called out in a loud voice, "Lazarus." That was when Lazarus walked out of the grave, and out of the cemetery. Doctors had no explanation for miracles like that.

Multitudes of the sick came to the Master after years of unsuccessful and expensive treatments. Jesus cared for them. It has been said that his touch and prayers of healing were more powerful than any other medicine. His fame naturally spread rapidly, far beyond Tiberias. He always credited his healing power to the heavenly Father.

For the past year I tagged along with the Master's disciples, the fishermen, only lately for different motives. Before, I wanted to learn how to catch fish, and to be like them. Now, I understand their deeper desires. They told me of their calling to be fishers of men. I wanted that too. They followed the Master believing him to be the Messiah, the one sent by the Almighty to draw men to God. Would God have a place for me in his kingdom? Recently I have learned more about men and their Lord and less about fish and lures. I fear, however, that I do not have the courage or the ability of the fishermen.

Perhaps someday, I thought, when I am grown, I will be like those men; I'll be better able to serve the Master. Surely, there will be time for that. But there was not. I did not see it coming. None of us did. I was only thinking about the Passover Seder our family would celebrate today. I did not expect he would be crucified yesterday. I knew he had critics but I never expected that!

As he hung on the cross, I longed for a gift that would make a difference to him. Anything. Food was useless. Weapons were impotent. What could I give?

His glazed eyes and slurred, almost incoherent speech indicated that help would be of no avail. Where were the followers who earlier clamored for his touch on the hillside beside Galilee? Where were those who had been miraculously healed? Where were the ones who had been delivered from demons? Where were his closest friends, those who lived with him and ministered with him for more than three years? Why were they silent at Golgotha, or absent? Why did they desert him in his hour of need?

I felt isolated and alone as I watched and listened. Worse, I was lacking any means of giving assistance in his hour of greatest need. I had nothing to give. I felt victimized by the religious leaders who, along with the soldiers, were a brigade of executioners.

Last year on the hillside my small contribution made a significant difference. Jesus took my lunch in his hands and blessed it, then miraculously distributed it to the multitude. There was more than enough for the thousands of followers.

When he reached out with his hands to touch broken bodies they were restored to wholeness. He lovingly held young children, or caressed old and feeble people, or calmed rebellious youths with just a touch. Then yesterday, those hands were tragically nailed to a cross; bleeding, mangled, impotent, and useless.

Whose hands will bring healing now? Whose voice will teach with his authority? What could I do? To whom could I go? Could John, Peter, or Andrew use their talents to contribute to his cause?

The fishermen, other than John were nowhere to be seen, and John was himself nearly incapacitated with grief, all the while ministering to Jesus's mother. But where were the other fishermen? They should have been at his side on the hill of suffering. Earlier they could have offered supporting testimony during the court trials. Then it was too late. The murderous rulers could not be diverted from their resolve to execute the Master.

What can I contribute now? I wonder if we can encourage the fishermen to support his family. Will his kingdom come on earth as he taught us to pray that it would? Perhaps the fishermen are on their boats today. I, too, will go and fish. It may not be much but it is something I do well. I pray that the Master may use me in some way. There must be something I can give to his kingdom.

A Sadducee:
The Self-Righteous Politician

Yesterday I bid a *shalom* of departure to the Nazarene. No tears were shed by me. I will not miss him and I suspect the majority of the people at Golgotha were also glad to see him go. Few of his followers remained at the end.

He was no friend of those who revere the Temple. He was always carping about the way the Temple sacrifices were conducted. I was not the only Sadducee to approve of the charges against him.

Our court is the Sanhedrin. I am one of seventy-one members who meet together in Jerusalem, sitting as a court of justice. Our traditions may be traced back to the time of Moses. Under the present Roman rule we have seen a resurgence of power, elevating us to our rightful status. Civil jurisdiction, criminal cases and administrative authority fall under our purview. Our rulings were inevitably at odds with the teachings of the Nazarene rabbi, and have been for some time. He acted as if he was the law.

I thought he took personal pleasure in antagonizing us. It is said that he often used our court as an example of sinfulness. How could he be so judgmental? We have been the standard of correct behaviour for more than a millennium.

At the end, I concurred with the ruling of the court, which corroborated the convictions of each member. Favorable public opinion had shifted to him. We were cast in the role of heretics. The Nazarene denounced the way we administered worship. His judgments of our lives become a liability to our very existence. His radical teachings and practices could potentially overturn generations of Sadducean traditions.

I could not understand the devotion of his followers. In life as in death the Nazarene made pronouncements, which had no hope of succeeding. At the place of execution he promised resurrection for one of the criminals. In what some said was a prayer, he offered his spirit to God. How did he get people to follow his questionable teachings about spirits? Did he promote himself as a priest or prophet? The sign on the cross went farther, calling him a king.

What did his followers think of the prophets in our history? Moses was loved, even idolized, though of course from only an historical perspective. Isaiah was tolerated in spite of his dire and gloomy predictions. Amos was earthy yet extreme as is his statement, "For three times and for four you will know God's grace, but then judgment." Jeremiah revealed human compassion, while Ezekiel spouted fanciful prophecies containing weird visions. Then there was the one I considered to be the reincarnated Ezekiel: John the Baptist. He was definitely a strange man, with a questionable diet of insects and clothing of skins. His teachings drove away those who desired true spirituality.

They warmed to the Maccabees two hundred years ago after some initial scepticism. But "warmed" is too mild. The Nation's patriotic zeal was a consuming fire. Hordes enlisted daily as a handful of Jewish guerrillas shook off the yoke of the powerful Seleucid empire of Antiochus Epiphanes which sought to crush their religion. It was in this Hasmonean era that we saw the restoration of the desecrated temple in Jerusalem. Emotions ran high in support of a regained sovereignty in our ravaged land. Most important was a renewed national will for independence.

Yet, absolutely nothing compared to the agitating Nazarene. For the life of me, I cannot understand the allegiance of his followers. He is surely the most impractical insurrectionist in our history. I, and others in my party, tried to reason with him. He should have followed our example. We trimmed our doctrines and beliefs to suit our desired ends and objectives. He always seemed so preoccupied. Like other hot-blooded patriots he stirred the multitudes to rebellion. We tried to instruct his followers. And we warned them. Disobedience to the established order was bound to bring recriminations. Our land needs order and peace. History reveals our party is greater than any one individual. I confess no impediment to the severest punishment when a revolutionary Nazarene disturbs the relationship of compromise and collaboration between my party and the occupying forces. His make-believe teachings were absurd. Everyone could see he was out of touch with the real world.

Ours is the priestly party. We are a long-established and revered religious order. Critics may say we are more political than religious, but that is how we have survived. Everyone knows that. We always had great influence among the rulers, in distinction to the motley crew hanging on the coattails of the Nazarene. Many religious organizations view us with envy. Politicians emulate our character, while admiring our inroads into society.

We revere our name, "Sadducee." It was taken from our founder, Zadok, the Davidic high priest and colleague of Abiathar. With honor, high priests have claimed to descend from Zadok from the time of David to the present day. Our name represents all that is good and right. It is a name with historical validity, and profound significance— Zadok means "righteousness."

Scribes everywhere pay homage to our teachings. We deny the resurrection of the body as well as the unfounded belief in spirits and heavenly beings. Who truly believes the Rabbi's speculation of an afterlife? Those who say they do are ignorant, or misinformed.

Of course the *sine qua non*, the irreducible minimum, of our doctrines is the denial of immortality and the resurrection of the body. Our scholars correctly assert the soul dies with the body. The crucifixion yesterday confirmed our centuries-old teachings.

We are often linked with the Pharisees and the Essenes, but I reject that slanderous insult. The high priest always came from our camp— at least throughout the past century—and I predict it will be so for the next two millennia.

We are noted as leaders in the Hellenistic movement to initiate our people into the new realities of the modern world. Alexander of Macedon was embraced by our scholars. He brought education and enlightenment to the people. Greek reforms gave rise to a renewed national identity for us in this land. Yet, it was not a perfect world. Some zealots stirred up rebellion against the invaders.

We had nothing to do with the Hasmonean revolt when Judas Maccabaeus stirred our national zeal, though it did give rise to the formation of our "union" so to speak. From the ashes of rebellion our Sadducean party was formed.

Those rebels, the Maccabees, were solely supported by the Hassidim, who happened to be the forerunners of the Pharisees. But Maccabean influence among the people was infectious, instigating vocal criticism from the leaders and political unrest.

I categorize the Pharisees as too rigid and self-righteous. I wonder what motivates them. I wait for them to be destroyed by their own impossible expectations. Typically they strut around in their garish, flowing robes, putting on a show for those they consider to be lesser pilgrims. Is it any wonder that the Nazarene was incensed by their professed righteousness? His consternation was of no consequence to us—at first.

Then in a moment of wild delusion he claimed to be the Messiah! The citizens who followed his teachings were uncontrollable. Next, a few religious leaders tagged along with his disciples. If Tiberius hears of widespread belief among the Jews in the coming of a Jewish king who would rule the world, his Roman Legions would be commissioned to quell the upheaval. How would he react if he knew some of the Nazarene's followers were promoting him as the Messiah? Very soon the privileges enjoyed by the Jews would be wrested from them. I also admit, sadly, the influence of my party would subsequently evaporate.

Sadducees have survived twenty generations of Phariseeism. That is a rare accomplishment. We are as much a part of the temple as those religious leaders. And we were elated when the rabbi from Nazareth judged their hypocritical posturing. We reject, out of hand, changes introduced by our opponents unless such changes find support in the words of the Torah.

Our leadership correctly confronted the Nazarene rabbi on his questionable relationship with the Temple. The officers will not forgive his outrage last year when he disrupted our worship. His tirade, which some followers labelled, "cleansing of the Temple", appeared to be motivated by petulance. He should have been told the righteous standards are set by the Sanhedrin.

I faced him one day and asked him about his disturbing actions which riled the merchants in the Temple courtyard. He answered with a question, "Do you not think this is my Father's house?"

Was he speaking in riddles? Proudly, I countered, "The Temple is our domain and the Torah is our lifeblood." Everyone knows how firmly connected we are to the synagogue. We draw the bulk of our support from the priesthood. I am more conversant with Temple affairs than he.

The rabbi did not hear me. Instead he spoke of commandments recorded in the Book of Moses. He challenged me to "Love the Lord your God with all your heart and with all your soul and with all your strength." When I mentioned the indignation expressed by the Temple staff he proclaimed, "You shall have no other Gods before me."

Many of my friends in the council were angered by his attitude. From that point we attempted to plot his demise. Avraham, who chairs our meetings, thought it best to charge him by using technicalities of the law. Surely, the Nazarene's knowledge of the proceedings of the Council is inferior to ours. Simon reminded the brethren that no individual is above the law. We unanimously agreed.

I thought the better approach would be to produce a record of the Rabbi's inflammatory heresies. Many of his statements about the Temple bordered on libel. He threatened to destroy it! I argued that if we heard these threats proclaimed before the whole Sanhedrin there would be a predictable outcry for revenge against one who belittles our Temple and our traditions. Then if we could get the politicians to act, and the courts to listen, he would be compelled to bow to our judgments.

Surely the Nazarene's followers must envy our expertise in financial matters. We have always laid great stress on the ceremony of sacrifice. Some may think us opportunists but in reality someone has to provide for the sale of sacrificial requisites. There will always be a need of tables for the money changers who convert ordinary coins into shekels for the sanctuary. From this we have derived our rightful profit. What if this seems irreligious? At least we are unmarked by the pride and hypocrisy that saturates the Pharisees. It leads me to think that the Nazarene should align himself more closely to the Pharisees. Like them, he too emanates an air of righteous behavior in contrast to other rabbis.

Where did he get the audacity to denounce us? We have influence among the rich while the Nazarene drew his admirers from the poor. How can the lower castes support his cause? It is another example of an impractical strategy from a simple laborer. None should have taken him seriously. If one cannot garner support and leadership from the rulers of the nation how will the foot soldiers follow?

It has been said, "The whole world has gone after him." Really? Where is he now? What is the state of his kingdom? Who can find his army? His legislative assembly is non-existent. His laws consist only of vague promises which are meant to attract interest but have no lasting impact.

A guard at the cemetery—I cannot imagine anything more futile. Those who "rest in peace" are unable to destroy our peace. The dead are not coming back. They are gone forever. By definition the body cannot be raised. It is a known fact. The Pharisees, Pontius Pilate, and the Nazarene rabbi, are all mistaken. Had they attended to the basic elements of our history and education they would have embraced this truth: there is no resurrection.

Compare his moniker, Yeshua or Joshua. In our nation his name is as common as sand. There is little to distinguish him from the hundreds of others called Joshua.

Contrasts between his followers and our following reveal the discrepancies. The history of my party goes back one hundred fifty years to our emergence during the second temple period. The Nazarene was barely 33 years old when he met his demise.

Secular history is on our side, as is financial history. Our management of business is unsurpassed. Our political system works. His problem is he never learned to work with the established leaders. His combative attitude was counterproductive. His disciples boasted about a cleansed worship space, but the merchants eagerly re-established their rightful businesses as soon as the rabbi left the premises. What was the point?

He could have used crowd support to his advantage. Instead he lost the majority of his followers who disagreed with his policies and programs. At the end he only had twelve discouraged followers, and most of them deserted in the final crisis.

Yesterday as he was dying I heard him gasp. "It is finished." It is over. We are done with him. He will no longer be the central item on our Council's agenda.

We have won! It is finished, as he discovered at last. We are through with his name and his influence. He will soon be ancient history. I am sure his few followers will simply fade away.

Mary Magdalene:
The Enraptured Devotee

It has not changed much, really: The nearby, fickle lake, teetering on the edge of sudden storms; the hardscrabble hillside falling away to the north; the sleepy village within strolling distance of the water; the residents anxious to get on with life as usual. We first met here, at Magdala. My town is on the northwest shore of the Sea of Galilee, nestled beside the road midway between Tiberias, beside the Lake, and Capernaum, on the north shore.

We met in town and the contrast was immediately obvious. Jesus had everything going for him. I was confused, and a pitiable disaster, unfit for society, and unable to relate to others. My home was inhospitable at best. The taste of abuse was constant, so I fled to the streets or camped in caves. Some deemed this way of life a personal right or freedom. For me it was an escape. Some of my companions thought our living conditions were acceptable. I knew there had to be a better way.

As though guided by some unseen influence, I felt my life was not my own. A foreign entity or force impacted my behaviour. Incapable of rational decisions, I wavered with every whim of my deluded thinking. Friends remarked on my tortured appearance, brought about by years of cruel abuse. You needed only to look at my anguished face to observe the inner turmoil. Wild, dilated eyes, glassy and unable to focus, revealed the chaos in my soul. Outwardly, my matted, stringy hair and dirty dishevelled clothes were signs of a life gone wrong. My face, distorted by distress and pain gave further evidence of demonic influences.

Then I met Jesus. Was it coincidence? Not a chance. I have since learned that God leaves nothing to chance. Jesus accepted me without judging my appearance. Memories flood my mind of the miraculous changes he brought into my life. He delivered me from my enemies, and from myself—the rebel self of the past.

Jesus, the deliverer! I am struck by how much Jesus loved them all: the poor, the sick, parents, children, bureaucrats, critics, the scribes, the military, the religious leaders, and his marginalized, wavering followers. Far too often these people chose to reject his love and care. Once I was among them.

I recall one sweltering day near Galilee. Jesus had been invited into a humble home to teach about the kingdom of God. His visit was no surprise to the neighbors. The whole town arrived, trying to squeeze through the narrow doorway. The poor folk in tattered clothes pressed forward, closing in on him. I caught glimpses of children peeking between the robes of curious, judgmental leaders, attempting to view the Master's face. Glancing out the window at the tiny courtyard I spotted Mordecai, the merchant, and Rabbi Yehuda. Many elite citizens from uptown strutted through the restless crowd, wanting to be seen. Eleazar, the priest, and several of his contemporaries surveyed the company that overflowed the house, spilling into the street.

Deep in my heart—my recently converted heart—I felt a twinge of pain at the sight of religious men in immaculate robes. I call them "impostors." Once I was vocal in my disapproval of their charade. Their faces expressed scorn as they beheld the helpless wretches shoving impatiently toward the Master in the tiny house.

I was backed into a corner by the pressure of the crowd, but was close enough to Jesus to see he still had room to breathe. Peter and John took up positions which allowed them to scan the surging crowd. They linked arms, with other disciples, as a protective barrier in front of the Savior, fearing he could be crushed by the over-enthusiastic throng. We were all perspiring heavily from the effort to restrain the people. The closeness of the crowd, the stifling, humid air, heavy with odors of sweating bodies, was overpowering. Deeply suffering patients with open sores, and yapping, malnourished dogs, combined to create a scene of privation and disorder. How did he cope? A lesser individual would have caved in. Peter and John along with Andrew encircled the Lord shielding him from potential harm. They acted as a line of defense and as visible support for Jesus.

Suddenly a woman's sharp scream broke my reverie cutting through the raucous noises of the throng. Her words were a distortion of wild ravings, almost unintelligible. "This man is Jesus, Son of the most high God." From the back of the room she moved forward, arms flailing, shouting like a maniac. It was frightening. Confusion reigned in the house. Supporters encouraged this woman in need of healing to seek the Lord's touch.

Critics demanded her silence with ever increasing shouts of, "Shut her up." Grumbling enemies readily attributed her delusion to the influence of demons, implying Jesus's power was of the Evil One. The curious crowd begrudgingly parted as she forced her way through to the Master. Overwhelmed by her loud voice and determined actions, I clasped my eyes shut, praying. With hands in my lap I sat motionless, meditating on the power of Jesus. All the while I was caught up in the moment, remembering my own conversion from Satan to the Savior.

Images of my earlier life flashed before me: the fumbling, ineffectual doctors and their futile medicines. Nothing had worked. Side effects from the treatments compounded my illnesses. Too often those charlatans were simply taking guesses which affected my life. The counsellors were equally incompetent.

Wearing the masks of prophets, they routinely spewed forth platitudes. I despise them all with mixed contempt. Most of these men took money under false pretences knowing full well they had no answers for me.

Then I met Jesus! I truly met him, the one who had the cure for my ailments. I discovered him to be the way, the truth and the life. He had the answers, not in Magdala alone but in every city and town, and in every house.

I consider again that memorable day in the little house and the polarized attendees, shouting criticism or voicing allegiance. In the months I had been a follower, traveling with Jesus's disciples, I never became accustomed to the Pharisees' judgments or the horrific conflicts with demons. Even though I knew from experience and from divine assurance what Jesus could do, I remained cautious and in awe of evil spirits, yet was exhilarated by the demonstration of the supreme power of the Lord Jesus Christ, my Master, the Messiah.

That same day he rebuked the evil spirit in the woman which threw her to the floor leaving her limp and senseless. Jesus touched her face, and raised his voice toward heaven, thanking the Father for the healing she was to experience. His profound words of deliverance—"You have been made whole"—shocked the crowd. Some praised God. But others sneered in disbelief. I was both frightened and exultant by what I saw, especially when I thought of my former condition. I had been like her. But, praise God, now I am free!

I mused about the warmth of his touch. Jesus's hand on my body changed everything. I remember the demonic images cast out by Jesus. I still revel in the miraculous healing. I saw that the woman's eyes became focused with sparkling clarity. Jesus had again touched one out of whom he had cast a demon. A chill of delight coursed through me.

That day I instinctively stepped forward reaching out to steady the woman as she struggled to her feet. Emotions rolled over me, flooding my eyes with tears. There was a ringing in my ears. Through the mob noise I heard the same voice that moments earlier had raved so madly, now speaking coherently. "Thank you, Master. Lord, I praise you. You are my salvation."

I drew her toward me enfolding her in my arms, and held her in my embrace. We wept together, understanding our common past and the degrading, manipulative forces which had exploited us. Pushing back the tousled hair from her tired face, I led her away from the astounded crowd. In a distant glade I shared with her my own special story explaining my personal, deep gratitude for the Savior's healing touch.

Since Jesus commanded seven devils to leave, my entire life has been changed. My bound spirit was freed. My cramped limbs relaxed. My demeanor was transformed. The loving glance of his eyes became as welcome as the refreshing waters of Galilee on a warm day.

I will never be able to explain exactly what happened to me. The experience was mysterious and too miraculous to describe. But, I felt a burden of great foreboding removed, and replaced by deep personal peace. Only one person understood it completely, and now he is gone.

My desire, actually my need, was to stay close to Jesus. I learned from experience that I could not afford to minimize the power of Satan. Unless I kept near the Lord I had no defense against the Devil's attacks. On the other hand, if I followed the Master out of love and gratitude, I was victorious. So I became one of his close followers. It was infinitely better than wasting away on the streets of Magdala.

When a woman puts her faith in Jesus Christ he rewards that trust. However, that is only the beginning. If her faith is centered in him as a person a new relationship is born. I gladly gave him my faithful devotion, motivated by all he has done for me.

What a change! Once I was completely possessed; now I am totally delivered. Oh, how I wish I had been able to deliver him from the unruly mob at Golgotha. I stood aghast at what I witnessed: the betrayal, the denials, the trials, the taunting and torture. Did the Psalmist envision this event as he penned, "My God, my God, why have you forsaken me? Why are you so far from saving me, so far from the words of my groaning? O my God, I cry out by day, but you do not answer, by night, and am not silent…But I am a worm and not a man, scorned by men and despised by the people. All who see me mock me; they hurl insults, shaking their heads: 'He trusts in the Lord; let the Lord rescue him. Let him deliver him, since he trusts in him.'" (Psalm 22: 1-2, 6-8)

Did you hear him at the Place of the Skull? Amid the trauma and extreme cruelty his feeble voice proclaimed certain victory. I did not comprehend then, nor later at the tomb. I could not bear to see such indignities to his precious body.

Others were there with their own expectations, pondering the significance of his life and ministry. They began to prepare his body for burial. The process was interrupted because it was the Sabbath. Now we must wait until tomorrow. I stayed until the end. I was the last to leave, paying my respects.

Without Jesus my life will be meaningless. I wished yesterday to kneel before him and proclaim grateful allegiance. He was more than life to me. At the end I tried to minister to his needs, but I failed. The end came yesterday.

Today I will worship the Messiah among his discouraged people. Tomorrow I'll finish the embalming. His glorious body was battered beyond recognition. It was devastating. What a sad end to his wonderful life.

Nevertheless, the world has been changed through the power of his teaching. Lives have been transformed by his ministry and passion. I am changed! I know what I was and I know who I am; I am a sinner saved by grace. I am a woman loved into his kingdom.

Formerly unable to enjoy meaningful relationships with others, I am now part of a loving family of the Savior's followers. I am now transformed and infused with humanity. He is the Messiah, a prophet, king and my redeemer. He brought me from utter darkness into the most brilliant light. How ironic after the darkness yesterday at noon.

This world will never again see one like him. I was uniquely privileged to see and hear him, in intimate dialogue. My life has forever been marked by an exceptional experience of the Lord's healing power.

I was present while he taught us in parables. As a new convert my mind was alert to the implications of his messages. I saw my life reflected in the parable of the sower. The farmer scattered the seeds which fell on a well-trodden path. The seeds were trampled, and the birds ate them up. My life has been a well used and stony path.

Jesus suggested that some of the seeds fell on rocks, but as they sprouted they had no moisture and so withered. Regardless of my good intentions I was doomed to fail without a changed life.

Other seeds fell among thorns which grew up and choked the

sprouted plants. Jesus brought the air of life to me. (The good seed—Jesus must have meant his own life—sprouted and yielded a crop a hundred times more than was sown.)

Once I was blind to his teachings but he allowed me to see. He lifted my eyes to discern spiritual truths. Why can't others receive the vision? Some are lovingly attracted to the Lord and the wholeness he brings. Others, of their own volition, reject his identity as the Messiah.

Yesterday, at the cross, I saw that he does not mean much to this world. Today, I want everyone to know he means the world to me.

John: The Beloved Confidant

I do not know the moment it happened but I am certain of this: one day we did become close friends. Friendships are magical and mystical. Sometimes you gravitate toward another who thinks as you do, or whose values mirror yours, or who reaches out in friendship to embrace you as a person. At what point does the growing together become friendship?

Jesus was my friend. We were confidants. We shared our lives. We had the same convictions, interests, goals and passions. What did he see in me that led him to select me as his friend?

His knowledge was unsurpassed, while I am a rough, laboring fisherman. His wisdom was incomparable. I strove to discern his wise teaching and found myself intimidated by his insight. He was spiritually adept, conversant with the heavenly Father's will. I continued to search for God's leading. He prayed with power, entering into the very presence of Almighty God. I fumbled along, grasping for appropriate words as I addressed God. He taught with authority, astounding the most scholarly rabbinic leaders. I followed his teaching, but preferred to stay in the background, supporting others more competent in promoting his Kingdom.

Why me? Why not Peter, with his boisterous leadership and impulsive bravado? Unwilling to shrink from confrontation or conflict, he could have served as the Messiah's front man. Peter is the type of person to be established as the cornerstone of a kingdom, leading the way, promoting the cause, and gathering support. He was already well known to community leaders. The Lord, when aware of Kingdom promises, would have had an eager ally to carry the flag ahead of the parade. When Peter was convinced of the rightness of a cause, he would fight to the bitter end, brashly confronting every critic, quelling any protest. I yielded to Peter when we were together. He is an old friend and a partner in my father's fishing business.

Or why not my brother James, whose vocational skill made him a true leader in the community? James' involvement in the Synagogue and his spiritual hunger promoted his regular attendance at worship as he sought to implicitly obey the Torah injunctions. If the Pharisees had hearts as pure they would have no need to indulge in such blatant self-aggrandisements. James' influence has always been a directive for others aspiring to achieve right and righteous behaviour. He would have been the natural choice to be the Savior's closest friend.

Peter, James and I formed an inner circle with Jesus, and we saw many miracles that the others were not privy to. And, out of the three of us, the Master deferred to me. The Lord chose me as his dearest friend. The whispered murmurings in the group were passed to disciples' eager ears, and not always from caring lips.

Someone taunted, "He is the loved disciple." It was spoken in hushed tones and with rancor. The whispering made me uneasy, and self-conscious. I sought neither the title nor the position of honor. The musings heard as slurs and personal attacks. They knew not my heart, but Jesus knew. They ascribed impure motives to me and questioned what they considered to be an opportunistic allegiance, but the Master saw through the jealous gossip.

To the Judeans, James and I were less than ideal disciples. We are from Galilee, considered by others to be the backwoods of our nation, but they forget it is also the bread basket of the nation and the area of the country that epitomizes the designation "land of milk and honey." Overlooked by their diffuse criticism is the reality of the bounty from the Sea of Galilee.

James and I have fished these waters as young boys in our father, Zebedee's, boat. He and his father before him supported our families from their commercial fishing businesses, dating from the waning days of the Maccabean presence in the country. Peter also was part of the fishing community, indeed a partner in our ventures.

Peter, James and I saw him the first time as he was surveying the boats. Jesus was not distinctively dressed as a rabbi. Nor did he appear to be a religious leader. He seemed comfortable around boats and fishermen, fully aware of the concerns and the dangers of our work. Jesus spoke as one well familiar with labors of fishing. His hands showed the calluses of a man not afraid to work overtime to finish a job.

His physique belied his genius for debating religious doctrines, and his acumen for wise teaching and perceptive pronouncements. He was the perfect example of one who could capture the attention and elevate the aspirations of a bunch of fishermen who were seeking basic answers to life's profound questions. I am sure this world has never known a teacher with such a grasp of divine truths. Further, he was superior to my namesake John the Baptist who led a mini-revival earlier in the year.

I was one of John the Baptist's two disciples who followed Jesus. Andrew, Simon Peter's brother was the other one linked with John's group of followers. Andrew lived near us in Capernaum, meaning easy access to the fishing grounds in Galilee. While mending our nets at the dock we chanced upon Jesus of Nazareth. Actually, it was the other way around. It now appears to have been a kind of planned spontaneity in concert with the Master's divine will. His stumbling across us at the fishing dock was no accident.

Jesus called us together, his very presence commanding respect. His vision was contagious and his bearing was unlike any other in our community. Immediately I was compelled to listen and more, to obey. I decided to follow Jesus which meant my father would have to pick up my share of the labors. Peter, Andrew, and James agreed with my decision and followed also, though not with such initial enthusiasm. Why were they not enraptured by the Lord?

The challenge he addressed to us beside the boat, was being lived out in the reality of daily experience: we became part of a group of disciples, following his wise teachings and insights, and attracting other followers. Spiritual growth was the essence of his plan for us and, moreover, for the whole of his creation. He viewed physical infirmities as temporary detours on the road to spiritual wholeness.

His teachings distinguished him from all others in history. Rabbinic opinions fell woefully short of his divine knowledge. Philosophers and scholars bowed to his unfathomable intelligence, and yet he masterfully communicated with all levels of society. From children to the most elderly, the Master's lessons were embraced, loved, honoured and respected. As I listened to his teaching I discerned eternal truths formed before the foundation of the world. His words typified his work. Jesus was the revealed Son of God.

Vital spirituality was modeled in his lifestyle. Daily communion with the Heavenly Father was as natural to him as breathing. He lived out Isaiah's prophecy in fulfilling detail:

"The Sovereign Lord has given me an
instructed tongue,
to know the word that sustains the
weary.
He wakens me morning by morning,
wakens my ear to listen like one
being taught.
The sovereign Lord has opened my
ears,
and I have not been rebellious;
I have not drawn back.
I offered my back to those who beat
me,
my cheeks to those who pulled out
my beard;
I did not hide my face
from mocking and spitting.
Because the Sovereign Lord helps
Me,
I will not be disgraced.
Therefore have I set my face like
flint.
and know I will not be put to
shame." (Isaiah 50: 4-7)

We were well-versed in this prophecy but ignorant of its application. Eager to follow our Lord, we too sought the will of God in daily disciplines of study and prayer. The Master taught us from the Holy Scriptures to acknowledge the Messiah. Reluctantly we realized Isaiah's teachings meant a suffering Messiah. The depth of suffering was greater than we had ever imagined. It hurt me so much to see my Lord, during his last days, brutalized at the hands of sinful men.

It is no exaggeration to say one day he was transformed before our very eyes. On the mountain his usual heavenly communion became an extraordinary experience with Elijah and Moses joining in. Jesus emanated a divine presence I had not witnessed. Peter, James, and I were forever affected by his holy demeanor. Many other life-altering experiences indelibly affected my life in the all-too-brief spiritual training with the Lord.

I am no longer what I once was, when catching fish near Tiberias. I know not how or when my life turned around, but I was changed. Did he see me as I was, or as I was meant to be? Surely, he saw my potential for his Kingdom when we met by Galilee. In those days I was a typical fisherman, brawling and boisterous, ready to fight and mix it up at the slightest provocation. Peter was worse. Regardless, the Lord saw in Peter, as in all of us, the potential rather than the problem.

Peter and I were sent ahead by the Master to make arrangements for the Passover Seder. Though every detail was known beforehand to him, it was all a mystery to us. I knew better than to question him even though the intricacy of the details seemed dire and improbable. A pall of impending sorrow gripped me throughout the meal. Joyful celebration was supplanted by a deeply-felt solemnity.

That night, the exquisite joy of intimacy with the Lord was tempered by an aura of veiled reflections. Judas Iscariot, long an irritant in any discussion about the Kingdom, was most antagonizing, pushing in to sit next to Jesus. In thinking back, I see that the Master was seeking to communicate significant truths to us. I did not realize then that this would be his final opportunity.

I am embarrassed by my weakness in the Garden of Gethsemane. I should have been strong for him in the hour of his greatest need. He innately understood God's divine will and program, and had often attempted to teach us to await the coming of the Kingdom. Why had I been blind and deaf to his Messianic identity? The evidence was clearly presented by the Prophets. John also pointed directly to his cousin as the fulfillment of prophetic promises, calling him, "The Lamb of God who takes away the sin of the world."

Jesus's prayer was a plea for the Heavenly Father to deliver him from drinking the cup of sorrow. Included was his plea that his followers be united in faith and love. My heavy eyes clouded my perception. I regret that my penchant for prayer was overruled by sheer physical exhaustion.

He returned from the inner recesses of the Garden, where he sought the refuge of communion with the Father, and found us asleep. Not joined in prayer. Not covenanting to empathize with him in trial. Not vowing to defend him before the Council. Not awaiting his discerning pronouncements. I was asleep.

The trials, torture, and execution were more than any civilized being should bear to witness. It would be too gruesome for one emotionally detached, let alone for his close companions. And think of the trauma to his mother and close relatives. His friends and followers deserted him at the end. Was it because of the profuse blood-letting or revulsion of the death squad? Did his loved ones fear for their own safety, seeking distance from any taint of alignment with Jesus? Were his disciples overwhelmed by the inhumane treatment of their friend? Had his friends' dashed Messianic expectations soured their resolve to work for the Lord and his imminent Kingdom?

He was my Lord. I could not desert him even if my own life were imperilled. My family and I were well-acquainted with the High Priest, Caiaphas, so I moved around his premises with ease. Peter's impulsive bravado turned into empty promises during the trials. Peter and I followed Jesus into the palace of the high priest. I went into the High Priest's courtyard along with Jesus while Peter stood outside at the door. I spoke to the doorkeeper so Peter was invited into the house, but only to have a confrontation. When questioned by a servant, he denied that he knew Jesus.

I was not similarly interrogated, although had I been I would like to think I could have endured the test. He was my light, my life, my Lord, my King. It is unthinkable that I would leave him amid his trial, even though there was precious little I could do to affect his rescue.

He had tried to teach us about the Kingdom, the many prophetic fulfillments of his life and death, and his Messianic identity. He told us that his suffering and death were foreordained. I had missed the truths at the Seder and, later, in the garden. Was I imperceptive, or had my heart overruled my thoughts?

The cross etched its horrific aura above the skyline of Golgotha. One would think the bloody scourge was enough injustice. This Roman tool of torture is infamous for its excruciating injuries. Scourging quickly removed the victim's skin and flesh from his back and shoulders. Deep lacerations, torn flesh, exposed muscles and excessive bleeding had left Jesus half dead. I wondered if the lashings would claim his life before the cross could exact its bitter toll. Still, Jesus had intimated that the suffering servant must endure the cross before he would enjoy the crown. The Messianic promises were being fulfilled.

Mary stared blankly in deep shock, not comprehending the violent depravity directed against her son. Her feeble lips were trembling in fear and loathing of the executioners. She appeared a pathetic victim of the sin of wicked men, both unable to view the horrible afflictions yet unwilling to turn her loving gaze from the extensive brutality meted out to her son, Jesus. Her irritated, bloodshot eyes, long since bereft of tears, were unable to encompass the horrors of her son's tragic dying.

My selective hearing shut out the profane curses from the tortured criminals and the sadistic executioners. Lost in the din were the scarcely audible mumblings from the bloodied lips of the Savior. Among the death throes of the dying I heard him cry for physical relief from the ravages of thirst.

He responded to the final appeals of the two criminals. He forgave the savage executioners. He communicated intimately with his Heavenly father. He loved me to the end.

A spear finished the vulgar wickedness of the cross, but his heart was broken long before. As he observed his mother's traumatic suffering, his compelling love ministered to her. Nearing the cross, I struggled to discern his barely audible message, interrupted by frequent pain-filled gasps of breath.

Seeing his mother beside me, Jesus was prompted to speak in love, "Dear woman, here is your son," and to me, "Here is your mother."

Why did he leave us now? His ministry was incomplete. Was he aware of the torment I felt hearing his final words, reacting to the mob's indignities? His suffering was unimaginable. And I was unable to ease his pain. Then he admonished me to care for his mother, care without the limit of time. It may require tending to her needs within my home for the rest of her life. Am I able to obey his command?

Soon after, the awful injustice was mercifully completed according to the prophesied Scriptures, when the all-wise Savior proclaimed, "It is finished."

It will never be finished for me, or for Mary. I know it had to be, but I have lost my dearest friend. He promised to send a comforter after he ascended to the Father. I need his comfort and his counsel. The Lord promised, "Unless I go away, the Counselor will not come to you; but if I go, I will send him to you. When he comes, he will convict the world of guilt in regard to sin and righteousness and judgment: in regard to sin, because men do not believe in me; in regard to righteousness because I am going to the Father, where you can see me no longer; and in regard to judgment, because the prince of this world now stands condemned." (John 16: 7-11)

His work is completed. My forever friend has gone to the father. I will pray, and this time I will be alert and vigilant waiting for his Comforter; and for his return.

Lazarus: The Resurrected Friend

God has had his hand on my life for as long as I can remember. I do not recall my first encounter with Jesus, but I know it was not by chance. Daily there are many intriguing reminders that the Lord is in control of every detail of my life. I am sure he is the Son of God.

Believe me, he is my ever-present help, my fortress, my Savior. O how I love to read the Psalms in all their grandeur. I note the interplay of arguments between God's people and the criticism of the ungodly. The Psalmists recount numerous contrasts between the true, personal God and the proliferation of idols abounding around us.

"Why do the nations say,
'Where is their God?'
Our god is in heaven;
he does whatever pleases him.
But their idols are silver and gold,
made by the hands of men.
They have mouths but cannot
speak,
eyes, but they cannot see;
they have ears, but cannot hear,
noses, but they cannot smell;
they have hands, but cannot feel,
feet, but they cannot walk;
nor can they utter a sound with
their throats.
Those who make them will be like
them.
and so will all who trust in them.

O house of Israel, trust in the
Lord—
He is their help and shield." (Psalm 115: 2-9)

What idols can heal the sick? Which can open eyes of the blind, or enable the lame to walk? Who can raise the dead? Consider: Raise the dead!

How I praise the Eternal for my parents. I was blessed to be raised in a godly home. My mother and father were devout followers of the Covenant God of Abraham, Isaac and Jacob. As a testimony to their faith they called me "Lazarus." It is a name derived from the Hebrew, Eleazar, combined with a Greek termination meaning "God has helped." Their spiritual leadership directed me to worship on holy days. I was encouraged to read, and indeed to recite passages of the Torah.

I revelled in the history of our people. I marvelled at the miracles of God's intervention and the wondrous displays of his grace. *Baruch ha Shem!* Blessed is God's Name, for placing me in my home and for my loving parents. They prepared me to see and recognize truth when confronted by it.

My sisters initially contacted the Messiah. Actually, it was Mary, no doubt during one of her wistful wanderings. Clearly, I now understand, it was no mere coincidence. God's timing is as supernatural as his divine word; his wisdom is as infinite as his being. He has designed his resources to obey his voice, whether the wind and the waves or the cattle on a thousand hills. God's person is revealed and his purpose is fulfilled in the lyrics to Asaph's song:

"Hear, O my people, and I will
speak,
O Israel, and I will testify against
you:
I am God, your God.
I do not rebuke you for your
sacrifices
or your burnt offerings, which are

ever before me.
I have no need of a bull from your
stall
or goats from your pens,
for every animal of the forest is
mine,
and the cattle on a thousand hills.
I know every bird in the mountains,
and the creatures of the field are
mine.
If I were hungry I would not tell
You,
for the world is mine, and all that
is in it." (Psalm 50: 7-12)

I am amazed at the scrupulous religious leaders, the Pharisees, whom I see as charlatans who fail to contrast favorably with the aura of his wise authority. Their futile posing is as absurd as their ill founded faith in idols—mute, cold impotent—in comparison to the Almighty. How ridiculous! Our prophets exhausted that illogical argument centuries ago, including Isaiah when he contrasted man's idols to the omnipotence of Almighty God.

"All who make idols are nothing, and the things they treasure are worthless. Those who would speak up for them are blind; they are ignorant to their own shame. Who shapes a god and casts an idol, which can profit him nothing? He and his kind will be put to shame; craftsmen are nothing but men. Let them all come together and take their stand; they will be brought down to terror and infamy."

Isaiah further cautioned idolaters, "Remember these things, O Jacob, for you are my servant, O Israel. I have made you, you are my servant; O Israel I will not forget you. I have swept away your offenses like a cloud, your sins like the morning mist. Return to me for I have redeemed you." (Isaiah 44:21-22)

Then there was Rabbi Shabbathai Gueri, a quack with a loyal but deluded following. He was a self proclaimed Messiah who promised to bring a millennial kingdom to earth. This would occur when the world was either exceedingly good or exceedingly evil. Since the latter is more easily attained, he admonished his people to be indulgent, licentious, hedonistic, profligate, and corrupt. He, like so many other pseudo-Messiahs embraced other cults and turned against our people.

Instead, we should joyfully listen to the words of the Lord:
"The ransomed of the Lord will
return.
They will enter Zion with singing;
everlasting joy will crown their
heads.
Gladness and joy will overtake them,
and sorrow and sighing will flee
away." (Isaiah 51:11)

My family was privileged to experience friendship with Jesus. He was a guest in our home. He compelled attention as we hung on every word. Each conversation was a glimpse into royalty and godliness. He had vision to see the large picture, but was unstressed by minute details. Amid my sisters' sibling rivalries he remained unflappable, ever in control. When the squabbling got intense and personal, Jesus stayed in character. Imagine the God of the universe being privy to a family fight. It was embarrassing.

You know how petty girls, sisters, can be. These two make a striking contrast. At times it is hard to believe they have the same parents. They are poles apart, yet each loves the Lord in her own way.

Martha is the domestic one. I say it not as a criticism. She is valued and appreciated in our home. Any home benefits from the gift of hospitality and our home is no exception. Her caring concern for guests reveals itself in practical ways, by tending to their needs, and making them feel welcomed. I wish she would be more accepting of Mary. She doesn't get it. God has made us and given each of us special gifts.

Martha and Mary are unique in the Lord. It doesn't matter that

Mary has her head in the clouds and her heart in her hands. God's purposes will be worked out in each of their lives. I love them both. And, so did Jesus. He freed them, and elevated their eyes to see eternal values. He revealed himself as the Messiah. We believed him then, and now.

Jesus was human in every sense of the word. He got hungry and thirsty, felt tiredness and anger, and became irritable and discouraged. None of those responses negated his loving care or his balanced emotions. He was learned, articulate, and wise beyond imagination.

The Savior loved to come to our home. For him it was a spiritual and an emotional oasis. He made us feel as if we were actually giving him something of value, a precious gift. God has richly blessed us, so of course we could afford to entertain him, yet it felt as though we gave so little.

The perfume was costly but he was worth far more than any gifts we might offer. Mary's offering of spikenard in an exquisite alabaster jar was given confidently and genially without any reciprocal expectations. Few perfumes could compare in cost. I am told it was taken from a selection of pink blossomed plants in Northern countries near the Himalayan Mountains. Tediously transporting the precious cargo along trade routes by camel caravans added to the financial picture. In total, it equalled most people's annual incomes. Still, you cannot put a price on love. Jesus didn't. I learned long ago we cannot out-give the Master.

I grew to love him more deeply over the final months. That love was severely tested, however, by my death. I was devastated! Why had he not come to me sooner? Was he too distant to handle the travel arrangements? Did he misread the urgency of my sisters' message? Was he too unheeding or uncaring?

It hurts me to contemplate such questions. In the past he had arrived at a moment's notice. What happened to cause his delay? Where was he when I desperately needed him?

As I weakened, my emotions were in turmoil. I knew the grim reality of impending death. The doctors had speculated recovery but eventually admitted my case was beyond medical intervention. They knew of nothing that could alleviate the pain or cure my illness. I confess to being bereft of faith at the end.

Do not ask me my whereabouts those four days in the grave, nor question my experiences. I am unable to express my thoughts and visions. Others have spoken hypothetically of out-of-body experiences. Uncertain if my experience qualifies, I know my vocabulary falls short, and I have not the capacity to describe the indescribable. Besides, this world seems too crude and immoral to bathe in heavenly splendour and beauty.

I stand aghast as to why he should crown me with the miracle of resurrection. His call to me, by name, was more powerful than any compulsion in life. In reflection, I perceived his identity as the Son of Man and the Son of God. He was the Lord of life and death. Like Job I raised my voice to the heavens:

"If a man dies, will he live again?" (Job 14:14)

Am I the firstborn among his resurrected ones? I am reminded of Job's assurance:

"I know that my Redeemer lives,
and that in the end he will stand
upon the earth.
And after my skin has been
destroyed,
yet in my flesh I will see God;
I myself will see him
with my own eyes—I, and not
another.
How my heart yearns within me!" (Job 19: 25-27)

In the divine act of resurrection, Jesus astounded his critics and strengthened his disciples. From that experience many sceptics, even among the Jews, understood the Prophets in a new light. According to his actions and teachings it must be concluded that he was the Messiah. My Lord and Christ will one day be acknowledged and worshiped by all these people.

Why was I selected to be the recipient of his attention and grace? His critics were dumbfounded to see me emerge from the sepulchre.

Their confusion turned to wrath, with Jesus as the focus of their hostility. Did he not realize the ramifications of his actions? The religious leaders had a valid complaint to take before the Sanhedrin. Any individual espousing civil disobedience deserves to be disciplined.

Jesus should have known they would turn on him, in what for him was a losing battle. They could not stand his notoriety. Their religion appeared shallow at best. Their pompous posturing was a sham.

Sadly, my resurrection apparently hastened his death. Making himself vulnerable by performing signs and wonders bred hostility among the people. However, he brought glory to God. Most in the crowd berated him. Some observers, however, chose to follow him. Hallelujah!

Today, critics are asking, "Is it over? Are we through with him? Can we get on with life?" I believe my life will never be the same; nor will Mary's, nor Martha's. Our lives were transformed the moment we met Jesus. I am learning daily how indelibly his image is etched upon me.

The chief priests are gloating today. What a sad lot! They are grasping for power that can never belong to them. God alone is Almighty. The Country is in disarray, confused by their emotions and dashed expectations which contradict his divine revelation.

His followers are scattered; their hopes shattered. The Savior is the only one who can pick up the pieces and make them whole. I believe God is in control. I am certain there will be a resurrection. I know it with every fibre of my being. This truth strikes me whenever I look in a mirror; Jesus will rise again! We shall live forever, he prophesied, "For he who believes in me will never die." (John 11:25)

A great resurrection rests just over the horizon. It will be a world-changing triumph at an instant when God's timing is perfect.

"I know that my Redeemer lives,
and that in the end he will stand
upon the earth." (Job 19:25)

Look at me. I am Lazarus, "God has helped." I will wait to see what happens. There will be a great miracle. If not today, it will be tomorrow, or the day after.

Caiaphas: The Dutiful High Priest

As the Nation's high priest I am custodian of all: traditions, public worship and the temple. I manage the temple property and finances, and I offer sacrifices. Once a year I am alone privileged to enter the holy of holies with the blood of atonement, the sacrifice of propitiation for the whole nation. Originally, this office had no secular authority, being regarded instead as the leading religious authority.

More recently my position has been envisioned as the leading authority whether secular or sacred. The leadership of this Nation and the continuity of religious life in Israel are under my purview. How God is worshiped, and all righteous conduct associated with worship are my responsibilities. Religion is not only a way of life. It is my career. I am Joseph Caiaphas, the high priest, accountable for Israel's welfare.

I believe in myself and my ability to finesse through political obstacles. Some truths are established forever—our priesthood and institutions, and, the temple. I must protect and preserve these at any cost by whatever means necessary. Dire measures are justifiable to achieve noble ends. Expediency may be required. So too, wisdom plays a part in our politically dominated day. If it sometimes involves civil disobedience or perjury, who shall judge? Is it not possible that one should die for the good of all the people? Shall a fanatical revolutionary win the day by destroying our institutions built over many, many years? Should we allow a young hothead preaching a spiritual kingdom to supplant the wise religious order in Israel?

At times the gloomy Galilean reminded me of the prophet Amos with his dire predictions of judgment,

"This is what the Lord says:
'For three sins of Judah,
even for four, I will not turn back
my wrath.
Because they have rejected the law
of the Lord
and have not kept his decrees,
because they have been led astray by
false gods,
the gods their ancestors followed,
I will send fire upon Judah
that will consume the fortresses of
Jerusalem.'" (Amos 2:4-5)

My advisors admitted the latest insurrectionist from Galilee was, like Amos, a prophet of sorts. In the tradition of our law he insisted on "renewal" as though the chief goal was for individuals to have new hearts. He was as off base as was the late John the Baptist. Pure subjectivism is always a fatal mistake with mystics.

For forty years the temple had been under construction. The Galilean's empty boasting was delusionary. He prophesied that he could destroy it and rebuild it again in three days. Visionaries have the capacity to stir up the naïve idealism of the common folk. A rallying populace inflamed by rhetoric can be highly unstable, and dangerous.

I recall the abhorrent patriotism that swept the land under Judas Maccabaeus. The Galilean is another self-styled Messiah appealing to a lost cause. It is more likely the true Messiah will arise from our priestly ranks. Prophets have their place, but it is carrying things too far when the temple is threatened. Someone had to step in to quell the insanity. I assert in God's presence, it is my responsibility.

Ever since Archelaus was deposed by Rome the Sadducees kept good order. A powerful, wealthy oligarchy from our most prominent families has controlled the institutions. Our councils evinced superb wisdom and a profound understanding of the times. Collaboration with Rome has been essential in easing the pressures of political leadership and retaining self government. Our Sanhedrin cunningly guides the various institutions as well as the common life in the nation.

What a pity it would be if one popular hero amid a vanguard of peasants managed to ruin it all. I am of the Sadducee aristocracy, conferred to the office because of astute planning, ambitious vision and financial skill. The sale of requisites for temple sacrifices has produced for me enormous wealth. Sheep, doves, wine and oil are necessary purchases for worship. The Galilean denounced those who made the house of prayer a den of robbers. Was he referring to me?

History of the priesthood sustains me. Foresight and political discernment have been my keepers. Did not Valerius Gratus appoint me? And have I not served longer than any of my predecessors? Five high priests ruled in five years before me. Yet, I was raised to office and have continued ruling now for more than a decade. I tell you, it takes expediency to survive these days. None of them had it, including Annas.

It is not without superior planning that I find myself as Annas' son-in-law. Even before Annas, his father, Seth, provided a political base when he was elevated to the high priesthood by Quirinius, governor of Syria. Reportedly, the parents of the condemned criminal traveled to Bethlehem years ago in obedience to Quirinius' orders regarding a tax issue.

My father-in-law's family benefited greatly from his connections. Each of his five sons was appointed as high priest, before me. His continued prominence is revealed by the order of reference. Annas is listed first in all official records. It irks me somewhat, for my rightful place currently should be at the top. I am the actual high priest. The crucified one should have been brought first to me after his arrest. Only when Annas failed to get cooperation from the accused was he sent to me.

After his arrest, Annas questioned the prisoner about his disciples and his teachings. It was a kind of informal confrontation, a preliminary meeting to gather material for a subsequent trial, if we needed it. Of course we had a trial. As head of the Sanhedrin, I thought it was correct to deal with the issue in house so to speak. The

Sanhedrin was the ruling body, even though I admit, aged Annas was the ruling spirit.

The criminal was brought to me in bonds for the ensuing interrogation. Weeks earlier I counselled the court to wait for the right time to confront the traitor. Then, when the opportunity was upon us, the sacrifice of the Galilean would rid ourselves of a dangerous rival. The Sanhedrin accepted my advice. The arrest of Jesus occurred according to plan. Witnesses were beckoned to address the court. Some called them false witnesses, which was a mere technicality.

In my court we plotted as one body, the elders, chief priests and Sanhedrin banding together in collegial complicity. The accused assumed an air of uncooperative detachment. His attitude antagonized the court. His growing fame and claims of kingship dominated our discussion spurring us to act. Voices raised in violent crescendo demanded his death.

A range of possible scenarios followed. Maybe public flogging would pacify the crowd. Others voted for the death penalty. All the while we heard, "But not during the Feast or there may be a riot among the people." I feared the vengeance of Rome, and the loss of my personal authority and prestige. I have staked my position on collaboration with Augustus Caesar, the Roman emperor.

Documentary grounds against the Galilean were scarce, even though many false witnesses came forward. Finally two gave evidence that would stand up in court. They cited him saying,

"I am able to destroy the temple of God and rebuild it in three days." (Matthew 26: 61)

I was compelled to confront him, "I charge you under oath by the living God, to tell us if you are the Christ, the Son of God."

He really infuriated me when he responded, "Yes, it is as you say." He made it sound as if I were agreeing with him.

Further heresy spewed forth in an implied threat, "I say to all of you: in the future you will see the Son of Man sitting at the right hand of the mighty one and coming on the clouds of heaven."

Stunned, I tore my robes, screaming "He blasphemes! Why do we need any more witnesses? Look, you have heard the blasphemy! What do you think?"

I was cognizant of injunctions in the Torah against defacing the high priest's robes, but I doubt these misguided people were knowledgeable about prohibitions of the law, although the Sanhedrin should have known better.

As with one voice the blood-thirsty, raucous mob echoed my conviction, "He is worthy of death."

The courtroom rapidly degenerated into an explosion of violence. They spat in his face and struck him with their fists. A profusion of jeers and ridicule intensified the murderous mob.

After the accused criminal was struck and battered, mocking voices challenged, "Prophesy to us, Christ. Who hit you?"

I did nothing to stop the travesty. What could I do? The criminal was guilty and definitely worthy of death, and the cursing multitude was out of control.

Some things are difficult to explain. How can a young man blind from birth recover his sight? He was well known in our district, so I can verify the facts of this case. When rumoured he could see for the first time in his life we summoned him to appear in court. Examiners verified his vision. We simply had to conclude we did not know how it happened.

But, the greater mystery was the reported raising of Lazarus from the dead, which investigators believed was an incontestable reality. That was the last straw, the final indignity to the court. The horde who gave credence to the tale would have made Jesus king on the spot. We were forced to admit he did many wonders which could not be explained away. However, proven sedition and revolution outweigh any alleged contributions of community kindness. The blasphemer had to be punished with the full forces of Jewish and Roman justice.

The procession into the city was something I hope will never be repeated. What disarray! It could not be tolerated during my reign. The menace of a new religious movement arose from the turbulence surrounding the Galilean. The chaos of the procession was disconcerting. My men said the Galilean was hardly an agitator, but he was an anarchist nonetheless. He had a combative aura about him, ready to attack established leaders.

We could tolerate his extraordinary piety which never hurt anyone. And, his doctrines were not especially heretical. But, to disregard the temple, the center of our religion, was a fatal mistake. How could he be the Lord of the temple when he threatened to destroy it?

I felt strangely uneasy in his presence. It was as though I, not he, was standing trial. I found myself making a defence. He cared not to defend himself whatsoever which troubled the judges. His flippant claims insulted us. I bore greater responsibility than any person on the judges' bench. I should be respected, indeed feared. The Galilean held our court, our rulers and our laws, in contempt. He also condemned himself in the court of public opinion.

I will admit, there was a point where I was exceedingly nervous. Although our court had rightly condemned the prisoner to death, the Roman government would not let us carry out the execution. They always insisted that they alone have the "power of the sword." Actually that worked to our advantage, since it meant that the prisoner died as a criminal by Roman crucifixion, rather than as a martyr by Jewish stoning.

So we had to go through the troublesome process of a trial by Pilate. We had to invent some new charges, of course, since blasphemy was hardly a matter of concern to Pilate. And we almost lost the case when Pilate declared the prisoner to be innocent. But, in the end we prevailed, possibly because we threatened to complain to Rome about Pilate's inept administration. It was a real vindication of our sound judgment and fair handling of the matter to hear Pilate join in condemning the prisoner and then direct Rome to carry out the execution.

As he hung upon the cross on the hill of Golgotha it was too late for appeals. I went along with several chief priests to survey the execution. I will admit there was something compelling about it all. He would no longer be able to boast about building temples.

One of the soldiers insisted Jesus was a righteous man, while one of the criminals asked to be remembered when the Nazarene came into his kingdom. To show the people they were being duped we shouted, "He saved others; let him save himself if he is the Christ of God." Of course, he could not. Thus the issue was settled forever.

Now he is gone and will soon be forgotten. In contrast, my name will live on as the protector of our religion, the one who saved our sacred institutions. No use thinking any further. Anyway, it is almost time for the afternoon sacrifice.

Herod Antipas:
The Corrupt Governor

I am a survivor. Say what you will, I have outlasted them all. Rigorous training in school contributed to my considerable success. Intense rivalries in my family played a crucial role as well. My father was no angel, preferring to solve problems swiftly even if brutal action was needed.

I have been governor of this godforsaken Galilee since my early twenties. Who else rose to prominence so quickly? Who can boast of such noteworthy successes as mine, including ridding the dominion of dangerous freebooters and renegades? Who can match my record of raising tribute money for the Roman government?

For thirty years I have been Tetrarch of Judea. It has never been easy. Years ago, somewhat fortuitously my family was forced by circumstances to temporarily leave our domain in the hands of the Parthians and Antigonus. In a final spasm of death throes of the Hasmonean house, Antigonus took Jerusalem by storm. He and his fellow rebel guerrillas also captured my uncle Phasael. Not surprisingly, that weakling took his own life by dashing out his brains against the walls of his prison. During this indignity to my family, my father was at Rome, honoured to receive the crown of Judea.

With raging, boundless ambition and the liberal use of the sword I was able to carve out my own vast empire to complement the territory established by my father. Under Herod the Great Jerusalem was secured in a mere month of fighting. In retribution the Maccabeans were completely exterminated. They are related to me by marriage;

87

Mariamne is the granddaughter of Hyrcanus. Those were bloody days. Antigonus and forty-five of his henchmen were sacrificed.

The high priesthood was subsequently bestowed on Aristobulus, another uncle of mine. Of course, criticism abounded, but what do these ignorant Jews know? I consider them akin to pigs and barbarians. My family was not swayed by those indecent passions of protest. After the crumbling dynasty of Maccabees accused us of favoritism, it is fitting and fair that my family was acquitted by a Roman court. I and my family are survivors.

The power and authority of the Herods is more than regional. Octavian of Rome was so impressed he issued a mandate to recover the country from foreign marauders. We have always espoused a pro-Roman administration, continuing to this day. No one else comes close to my father's record. Building the Roman port and military base at Caesarea was no small task. Nor was the temple to Augustus at Samaria. And, think about the splendour of the Herodion, the Herod family's personal fortress, prominently occupying the hilltop vista overlooking Bethlehem.

Both a fortress and a mausoleum, the Herodion could not have been built by less daring adventurers in the architectural community. This massive project required the removal of the summit of a hill. An entire citadel rests inside the structure encompassing one of my fortified palaces. The fortress itself consists of a double circular wall with four towers facing the four cardinal points of the compass. The outer diameter of the wonderful monument to greatness is a full sixty meters. Entrances in the encircling wall lead to the towers, underground chambers and reservoirs. My father was right when he ensured, "Nothing can touch us there."

Like my father, I have a passion for building, and for beautifying what has been built. I built the wall of Sepphoris and made the place my capital. I rebuilt Bethsaida and renamed it "Julia", after the daughter of Tiberius.

These bumbling Jews forgave my father for his many indiscretions after he built the second temple at Jerusalem. They begrudgingly admired his architectural abilities. And, they relished his tact as a diplomat. In a stroke of genius he suppressed the old aristocracy by marrying Mariamne, who was from one of their own families. Establishing a nobility of officials was logical and approved by the masses. Loyalty to Herod's house followed the founding of the Herodians.

My father built a solid foundation upon which I have further enhanced our fortunes. I have successfully advanced and elevated the name of Herod, which will be remembered in this land for many generations. An army of mercenaries protects all, people, cities and strongholds, and especially marvellous Masada.

Ah, Masada! It is a masterpiece of architecture and construction. It has stood for forty years and will continue for another thousand. An impregnable fortress, it is a place of escape from Jewish zealotry. I love to stand on the balcony of the north terrace and gaze in safety at the western shore of the Dead Sea. Or else, to meander along the expansive mesa of the upper plateau as I reaffirm peace for my family. There we are more secure than in this riot prone city of Jerusalem. Masada is surrounded by a casemate wall four meters wide. The outer and inner walls are strengthened by filling the center with rubble. More than 100 towers rise above the wall ranging in height from six to thirty meters.

Three gates offer access, yet provide complete protection. The gate on the east allows entry where the snake path terminates. The western gate allows access to the Western Palace, reached by a relatively broad flight of stairs. To the Northwest lies a water gate. Masada was planned for every eventuality. Water, more precious than gold, is supplied through a special trail at the northwest corner via the water gate, and securely stored in cisterns.

Encroachments by hostile forces are impossible. My food supply is equally inaccessible to potential enemies. Immense storehouses hold a valuable cache of staples and delicacies, amassed from trading partners throughout the world. As soon as I quell these unruly Jewish uprisings, I anticipate a regal feast at my palace.

Yesterday, and the preceding days and weeks, revealed a

populace of weaklings and sycophants. They are easily won by flattery and timely support. It was appropriate that our boundaries were extended by Rome. We live in troubled times.

Our victories over a handful of Arabians should have sent a message to the whole world, "Herod is a man of action." The Arabians were crushed. My father felt compelled to eradicate all remaining traces of Hashmonean power. Thus, Mariamne had to be dispatched. He confessed, she seemed once to love him, but later her criticisms became abrasive. To cover up he justified arranging similar executions of Alexandra his mother-in-law, and two of my brothers. They were all warned. Herod was one neither to be trifled with nor scoffed at. Our family lives by its own rules.

Over the years I have tried to win over these pig-headed Jews. Who has been more charitable than I during famines? Who has been more understanding about their insane prejudices? Then they fling in my face that I am a usurper to the throne of David. They may hope for my demise, but I defeated them all. Who are they to criticise my private family life? What do they know of the daily tensions confronting supreme leaders? Intrigues, feuds, even murder as a way of life are learned behaviors in order to survive.

The religious fanatics are best served by focussing on their own morality rather than to cast aspersions at mine. "He is wholly immoral," John the Baptist said. Well, I took care of that problem. Then this other moralist from Nazareth assumed John's position of prominence, preaching about the kingdom of God, thereby fomenting unrest among the people who are always ready to riot at the slightest provocation. He was overtly critical of those who did not subscribe to his moral code. The Herods are beyond his judgments.

Yesterday began with great promise. My home was readied for Passover. Syncretism is necessary when ruling these suspicious people, so I condescend to their religious quirks. I continue to maintain safe, impeccable relationships with the Romans, Arabs and Jews. Inevitably rabble rousers of every religious persuasion pass before my throne, seeking mercy. Their pleas and excuses wear thin by the time they kneel at my feet grovelling for a sympathetic ear. Hastily I judge them and cast them aside with merely a cursory dismissal.

The man called Jesus was not easily dismissed. He has been a thorn in the side of the Herods for thirty years. It is said his birth caused great concern for my Father. The law which required eliminating hundreds of babies was naturally unpopular. I suppose the crucified one was indirectly responsible. When he appeared before me I was given the opportunity to impose punishment on one who dared to oppose Herod. Was he ignorant of the fate of his cousin John the Baptiser?

The unforgettable confrontation with the accused criminal from Nazareth in Galilee was more troubling than Caesar's interrogations. For years, it seems I heard the folklore surrounding the crucified one, "He is a healer, a scholar, a magician." In my presence he adamantly refused to demonstrate his alleged psychic power. In fact, under cross-examination that doomed pretender did not have the courtesy to reply. He rudely dishonored both my position and power. Wordlessly he stared as though he could read my mind, and appeal to my deepest hidden suspicions. Was he judging me?

One of my notorious talents is my dogged determination. I control my life and my decisions, bringing about what is best for my well-being. The crucified one could have learned from me. Instead he unwisely chose his own personal hell. His actions and attitudes condemned him. He did not deserve to live. I was convinced of the correctness of my decision at the time. My choice was confirmed yesterday. Everyone could see it was his life or my lifestyle.

I sincerely hope his delusions were not adopted by his followers. His futile vision was typified when he said, "If you destroy this temple I will build it in three days." Did he know he was out of touch with reality? I am a builder. My family has left a legacy of indestructible buildings throughout this land. What has he built? Had he survived I would have challenged him to match his work against my fortresses; his skills against mine; his dwindling clan of friends against my national power; his three years of fame against my three decades of supreme authority. The deficient Galilean is now dead and gone, while I continue to rule.

The sign read, "King of the Jews." It irked me because I am the king. I have earned the admiration and respect of my subjects. The pathetic crowds wandered in disarray. His own men fled. It is just a matter of time before I am universally worshiped while his body rots in the grave. My legacy will continue on in history.

The surly grumblings of the prisoners and crowd were in keeping with the trauma of the event. But, still, I am troubled. What did the Centurion mean? His words were an enigma when he addressed the crucified as the "Son of God." Surely, he was mistaken. What did he see that I missed?

If there was a glimmer of truth in the Nazarene's ramblings I would have detected it. His raving, deluded followers made empty threats against me and my family, but without their leader they will now be more easily controlled. I will not be coerced by a misguided mob following someone who would usurp my throne. Still, the rumors about his body echo in the labyrinths and alleys of this city. His futile followers murmured that he would rise again. Just in case, I will order the soldiers to secure that grave.

Pontius Pilate:
The Ambivalent Coward

Do not think I am unaware of the rampant criticism today around the Praetorium. Every Roman mercenary has his version of it. "He was too weak to be his friend, yet powerless to be his enemy." Who can win facing that dilemma? Washing my hands was construed by the crowd as evasion.

Others claim he should have been released inasmuch as I declared him innocent of the charge of insurrection. They misunderstand the tunnel vision and dogged determination of these Jews.

What is truth? How does one assess proper government? Let any of them see through my eyes, experience my position of responsibility, and judge if there is a perfect solution. I will never be coerced by a mob. As for the charge that I yielded to political intrigue, well let's see.

Sejanus judged correctly when, on behalf of Tiberius Caesar, he appointed me to govern this frontier province. Sejanus received power and trust from the Emperor. His foot in the door came about on his father's recommendation as Prefect of the Praetorian Guard under Tiberius.

Subsequently, Sejanus inherited the job as head of the guard, whose chief duty was to protect Imperial appointees. He rose through the bureaucratic ranks to become a very influential kingpin in Roman politics. We need his supervision to police the multitude of enemies abounding in this nation. Sejanus ruled the Praetorium, the judgment hall of Caesar's court, as a dictator. I take comfort knowing that the Antonio Fortress is rendered a safe haven.

A powerful Parthian empire lies adjacent to our Judean border.

Seven decades ago their forces defeated the Roman navy. We continue to squabble with them over borders and boundaries of our empire. Currently, Parthian territory extends from Israel through Syria to the headwaters of the Euphrates.

Supervision here in Palestine requires a ruler with a strong hand to combat wide ranging powers of Parthian city-states. Until recently, I reported directly to Caesar in Rome rather than the governor of Syria up in Antioch. Rome scrutinizes this Israeli hotbox, ready to strike any and all miscreants.

Was there ever a subject nation like these Jews? Their fanaticism and zealous attachment to the land surely makes them unique. Why even the majority living outside the Palestinian wasteland, scattered throughout Asia Minor and beyond, make their voices heard in our local partisan politics.

In Mesopotamia a remnant is allied with Parthian power. Many Roman citizens have been unduly influenced by foreign religions. Parthians and their Persian predecessors blend a mix of Near Eastern cults into a kind of inclusive syncretism. Thousands of Romans on their annual pilgrimage to Jerusalem face real dangers of foreign conspiracies.

Only seventy years ago we suffered a disastrous defeat at the hands of the Parthians. Eighty years ago their military swept through Judea. Every Roman knows the incalculable importance of retaining Palestine as a buffer between the Parthians and our major granary in Egypt. Ruling in this nation is like doing hard time in prison. The Procurator must be tough handed to survive.

I learned to respect the mood swings of the zealots when I first came up from the capital in Caesarea shortly after taking office. My troops flew crimson banners depicting the Roman eagles and exhibited images of the Emperor. We nearly had a riot as Jewish guerrillas sought to establish their authority over occupying forces. They could not win. Their frail fighters paled in the face of our superior soldiers and military tactics. But we were never able to totally eradicate them, nor their influence among a patriotic people.

Since Sejanus has been dismissed I am required to report to

Antioch. My suspicions regarding the new Roman Consul, Lucius Flaccus, were confirmed by informants. He is in bed with the Herods, kowtowing to their political whims. Herod and his family were my nemeses for years, attempting to secure my reluctant support of their evil schemes. No one surpassed the ruthlessness of Herod the Great. No sane individual murders his wife and two sons.

I heard that back about the time the Nazarene was born Herod massacred all boys in Bethlehem who were under two years of age in a futile attempt to eradicate potential rivals to his throne. He was responding to rumors fomented by certain travelers from the east who followed a star to our land. They were seeking a king. Herod dealt with the problem in his own extreme way. That he could stoop to genocide reveals his unfathomable paranoia.

Now, Herod Antipas has been accepted as King of Israel by his party. It is another example of nepotism among rulers who believe might makes right. His deepest passion was his lust for his brother Phillip's wife. When he was incapable of camouflaging his evil actions he had that wilderness prophet, John the Baptist, beheaded for making an issue of his immorality.

Today, Herod Agrippa is set on succeeding his uncle. He is the current darling of the masses. I shudder, because I know how much he hates me.

As if that were not trouble enough for the Nazarene, he could not overcome the cunning of the chief priests. They are all from the Saducean camp, determined to end the Rabbi's life. The Herods, too, are supported by the Sadducees. Young Agrippa is gaining a following of Pharisees as well. The combined force of that power structure was impossible to overcome. What about me? Governing in this city demands keeping favour with every faction. I refuse to let the inexperienced Praetorian guard tell me how to do my job.

When I discovered Herod Antipas was in the city I sent the teacher to him, thinking I could mend some bridges and make political capital. Granted, it was a slight evasion, but after all, a Galilean comes under his jurisdiction. Herod did not surprise me when he sent him back. Antipas is a politician first and foremost. His career could not survive if he were deemed responsible for the deaths of both John the Baptist and Jesus.

It was obvious to me that the poor prisoner was innocent. From our initial contact he evinced an aura of blatant honesty. Yet, innocent or not, he did not have a chance. The infuriated rulers would have found in time some way to end his life. I could not envision a riot in the streets. It would have posed a greater risk to many more lives. Rome would remember the uncontrolled anarchy forever. The balance of political power would have been irrevocable. Any stable government necessitates making friends and placating enemies, which is no easy task in this country.

Wouldn't you know my wife had a bad dream about my challenging confrontation with the Nazarene? She begged me to have nothing to do with Jesus. She never before took a personal interest in influencing my judicial decisions. What did she know about him? Had she met him, or heard him teach? Regardless, women can be superstitious, and without sense when it comes to power politics.

My first recourse was the possibility of releasing a prisoner at Passover. Barabbas was one of the more notorious criminals, and most feared. He was not one who should be allowed to run loose in the land. Instead they cried out for his release. Mob psychology ruled the day. They chose to embrace Barabbas in their determination to crucify Jesus. Which one would they wish to welcome to their family table? They must have been aware of Barabbas' murderous past. Did they not envision the ramifications?

One more expedient came to me. I commanded the bloody scourge to be used, thinking I could appeal to their pity. Such whippings by the cruel hands of ruthless soldiers invariably reduced even the most stalwart of men to quivering cowards grovelling for mercy.

The world reveres the Roman scourge so fearfully as to call it the "horrible flagellation." The wooden handle to which several leather thongs are affixed is easily swung by hardened torturers. Pieces of bone and metal embedded in the thongs make the agonizing whip more effective. Victims receive the blows to the back, loins, or according to the wanton cruelty of the executioner, to the face. This punishment often resulted in the condemned losing consciousness or life itself. Roman citizens are spared such extreme torture, but I was not restricted in this case. As the flesh was torn from the prisoner's torso the mob's passions escalated.

In retrospect the gory scourging was a mistake. I completely misread the crowd. The sight of his blood elevated their rage. When Jesus appeared before them, his body shredded, I said "Behold the man." It was unavailing. Their raucous demands still echo in my ears, "Crucify him!" Sinister voices filled with murderous epithets rose to a crescendo. One wag in the crowd entreated me to consult Psalm 45:7. A nearby scribe quoted, "You love righteousness and hate wickedness; therefore God, your God, has set you above your companions by anointing you with the oil of joy. All your robes are fragrant with myrrh, and aloes and cassia."

Surely, the Psalmist was referring to the reign of a king rather than to my duties as a procurator. I readily discounted the fanatic's misapplied reference. Among the rabble were many who had dipped into the wine early in the day.

About this time a penetrating voice screamed, "If you let this man go you are no friend of Caesar." If someone had added, "You are no friend of Herod either," that's all I'd have needed. Suddenly I felt it had to be. As though my hands were tied rather than his, my decision was made. Against my better judgment, I pronounced him guilty and turned him over to the unruly mob.

When it was over, they asked for a couple of guards to be stationed at the tomb. I cannot imagine anyone wishing such dreary, boring duty. It seems totally unnecessary. But with all those Lazarus rumors still circulating, I humored them.

It is possible a sprinkling of fanatics might claim Jesus rose from the dead. Another scene in a cemetery and you know whose star would fade in Rome. My career cannot afford to take another hit. A military presence could do no harm, and would demonstrate my iron-fisted control of the situation.

Sure, I showed contempt for everyone involved in the unseemly trial. I mocked them when I washed my hands. They will never be able to blame me for the outcome. The priests, the Sadducees, the Herod's, and even my mercenaries have to admit I kept control amid incredible pressure. They can't judge me!

One thing troubles me yet, however. I am unable to forget the man, Jesus. I judged him, but somehow I felt him judging me. He refused to answer when I asked, "Who are you?" I could almost swear I saw a king standing before me.

Peter: The Impulsive Leader

Yesterday Jesus was crucified. I cannot come to grips with that reality. Just three years ago he called me from my fishing nets, beside my seaside hometown of Bethsaida.

My name is Simon, the son of Jonas. I am a fisherman, yet, leaving everything behind, I followed him. Was he aware of the sacrifices? My career is finished; the neglected, idle equipment mirrors my weakened muscles and softened hands—no longer brawny and fit. My family, not at all sympathetic, thought I had been a victim of a religious fanatic or a false prophet. In their opinion forsaking fishing was a most unwise business decision which affected the whole family.

I always felt that my primary place among the disciples was in return for my devotion. As a rugged individualist, I was used to leading the way. If others chose not to follow, that was their loss. I took life into my own hands. The disciples considered me energetic, action prone, quick to put often rash thoughts to words. Granted, I am impulsive and strong willed. In the fishing business I am considered a valued worker. No one accuses me of lacking self confidence.

James, John and I were Jesus's closest confidants. We comprised a kind of inner circle when Jesus conferred on us the privilege of an elite status. The Lord often unloaded his daily stresses and cares in our presence. It must have been my intense loyalty that brought the favour of intimacy with him. Our lives were entwined with his for more than three years. We laughed and cried together. We shared meals. We lived as the closest of friends, as family.

Our prayers reflected our same spiritual values. We were committed to similar causes, and energized by divine truths and insights. Jesus used us as a triple sounding board. It is as though he needed our opinions before sharing them with the other disciples. We became chosen beneficiaries of leftover theological crumbs neglected by the milling crowds. The unruly critics became increasingly difficult to control during the past several months as we tried to assist the Master.

We were uniquely privileged to behold his glory on the mountain when he was transfigured. I wonder how the other disciples felt when they were excluded from the divine revelation. On the mountain we saw his divinity shining through his humanity. God put Jesus above the level of Moses and Elijah, who appeared before us. The voice of the heavenly Father announced his pleasure in the Son's ministry.

"This is my Son, whom I love; with him I am well pleased. Listen to him." (Matthew 17: 5)

We were favored recipients of God's divine truth: Jesus was Lord of all. He was superior to both Moses and Elijah, the two greatest prophets in our people's history. Our Lord was the one foretold of Moses, "I will raise up for them a prophet like you from among their brothers; I will put my words in his mouth, and he will tell them everything I command him." (Deuteronomy 18:18)

That day confirmed my belief in him. We were witnesses of his majesty. An aura of dull light evolved into brilliance reflecting from his radiant face. A bright cloud enveloped us. Could it have been the *Shekinah* glory marking the visible presence of God with his people? He changed before our eyes, as the very hand of heaven transformed his humanity into a supernatural being. The intense image was of another world too ethereal for me to comprehend. The world of the present was emerging as real and tangible. Our enraptured senses could barely contain rational thought.

Our all too brief mountain top experience was discerned to be God's personal approval of the Master's Messianic identity. This divine sanction of Jesus's person was revealed in imagery that was holy and heavenly. I was ecstatic! Why was I accorded this exceptional gift from my friend? My closest friend was indeed my Creator, King, Master and Lord.

His world was so different from mine. Where I attempted to walk boldly into the unknown, he was in complete control. There is no better illustration than the time I walked on the Sea of Galilee.

I am a fisherman and the sea is my home. One night amid a squall I watched the horizon form an amorphous shape. It was the Lord! With a tinge of self-satisfaction I recognized him. Confident that he was in my world, battling the steep seas, roiled by a contrary wind, I dared him to call me unto himself.

I was wrong—it was not my world but his. As I began to sink I cried for help from the only available source—my Lord. Could I reach his hand? I scanned the distance from the boat and instantly saw my frailty. I was overcome by panic as I surveyed the life-threatening danger. I feared for my safety. He lunged for me and saved my life. His hand provided more than a boost over the gunwales of the boat. It showed his desire for my trust and faith in him.

The last few days have been excruciatingly painful for all of us. We agonized with Jesus in prayer in the garden. He ushered us into the deeper recesses of Gethsemane to intercede with him. None of the others were so privileged that night. James and John were tired to the point of exhaustion. I fought drowsiness since he needed my support, but finally my body succumbed to a lack of sleep. His sorrow-racked appeals to us late that night were both a figurative and literal wake up call.

With boldness I confessed him. Without restraint I manifested my loyalty by promoting his causes. For my actions I received his praise, but also his rebuke. He once queried, "Who do you say the Son of Man is?"

The other disciples were conspicuously silent. It was I who answered, "You are the Christ, the Son of the living God."

He was pleased with my bold statement. "Blessed are you Simon son of Jonah, for this was not revealed to you by man, but by my Father in heaven."

And to such a commendation he added, "And I tell you, you are Peter, and on this rock I will build my church and the gates of Hades will not overcome it." (Matthew 16:13-18)

He designated me "Peter", meaning the strong one, or rocklike. Continuing, the Lord confidentially revealed he had to go to Jerusalem, suffer there and be killed. All this would result in his resurrection on the third day. The cryptic confession left us astounded. What did it really mean? Was it a test to determine our discernment? Did he wonder about my strength to lead others? Was I seen as being disloyal? Was it an exaggeration of possible impending conflicts with the religious leaders? I boldly protested, "Never, Lord! This shall never happen to you!" (Matthew 16:22)

His response was not what I expected. Being aware of my propensity to speak before considering the situation, he did not praise my determined defence. Instead, his voice coarse with emotion, he dismissed me, "Get behind me, Satan! You are a stumbling block to me; you do not have in mind the things of God but the things of men." (Matthew 16:23)

I was horrified. My loving confession he construed as criticism. I simply sought to protect him. My motive was impeccable, I thought, but Jesus saw it as a selfish utterance, distinct from his Father's will. Though often bold I never did exalt myself, nor ask for special dispensations. Our friendship was honored. Still, it hurt me deeply to be linked as one with Satan.

I felt no comfort when others missed the meaning of his spiritual teachings. Jesus often taught truths about eternal life. Once in the synagogue in Capernaum he proclaimed, "I tell you the truth, it is not Moses who has given you the bread from heaven, but it is my Father who gives you the true bread from heaven. For the bread of God is he who comes down from heaven and gives life to the world." (John 6. 32-33)

He applied this truth to himself, "I am the living bread that came down from heaven. If anyone eats of this bread, he will live forever. This bread is my flesh, which I will give for the life of the world." (John 6.51)

The audience was not receptive. Arguments ensued, "How can this man give us his flesh to eat?"

Even many disciples grumbled in offense saying, "This is a hard teaching. Who can accept it?"

Form that time many disciples turned back and no longer followed him. Sorrowfully he turned to us, pleading, "Will you also go away?"

Typically, I spoke for them all, "Lord, to whom shall we go? You have the words of eternal life; and we have believed and have come to know that you are the holy one of God." (John 6:68-69)

Imagine: eternal life, holy from God. How could I have denied him in a dreaded moment of weakness? The temptation to hide at the trial was seductive. I do not comprehend the contradictions that rule the human heart. To stand one moment confessing boldly only to falter the next to the point of disavowing him, is totally inexcusable. I am damned by my denials and my ungodly cursing in the judgment hall.

At the supper he confided, "Simon. Simon, Satan has asked to sift you as wheat. But I have prayed for you, Simon, that your faith may not fail. And when you have turned back, strengthen your brothers." (Luke 22:31)

How did he know? How could he discern my actions and reactions which were unknown even to me? Did he envision my prophesied failure?

In great earnestness I replied, "Lord I am ready to go with you to prison and to death."

I truly meant what I proclaimed. Could he see my heart; read my mind? I was shocked to hear, "I tell you, Peter, before the rooster crows today, you will deny three times that you know me." (Luke 22:34)

I drew my sword when the soldiers encircled us in the Garden. Acting on impulse, I struck at any who appeared to be the foe. It was unfortunate for Malchus, servant of the high priest, whose ear got in the way. And, fortunately for everyone involved, my aim was as errant as my judgment. Typically, Jesus chose to heal him.

As was his habit in his ministry, the Master healed those who were in need. Usually his miracles evidenced his divine nature. Before he touched the infirm he often asked the patient if he wanted healing.

"What will you have me to do?"

Jesus wanted the ill one to verbalize faith. While concerned about physical suffering his priority was on spiritual wholeness. But, why aid Malchus? He was one of the Lord's night-time captors in the Garden of Gethsemane. I attempted to protect Jesus, striking blindly with my sword at the nearest enemy. Malchus lost an ear. Did Jesus not value my valiant defense?

Following the crowd into the hall of Caiaphas brought increased risk for me. I could be recognized by the soldiers, or named by Malchus seeking revenge. Twice a hostile maid confronted me.

"You are one of his followers aren't you? I can hear your Galilean accent."

She irked me both by her directness and her insolent manner. At that moment I craved obscurity, not notoriety, preferring to watch from afar to see what they would do with my Lord.

It certainly was not because of fear that I disowned him. I had already risked so much. Was it pride that made me shun identity with him during his hours of crisis? Without realizing what I was doing I had denied my Master. How could that have happened? My fickleness shames me even now. Where was my faith for which he had prayed?

Immediately after the rooster called out at the first light of the approaching dawn, Jesus's prophecy rang in my ears. At the same instant as the rooster sounded his wake up call, the Savior turned and looked at me, with a single look, making eye contact, without words passing between us. It became a defining moment. It was not much but it was enough.

Stumbling out of the congested courtyard, I hid my guilty countenance from the incensed mob. Had Jesus observed my inability to return his loving gaze? My eyes were blinded with scalding tears. Weeping uncontrollably, I blindly ran through the chaotic crowd, jostling the mob in my foolhardy rush to escape.

At the time I cursed Judas for his traitorous act. Yet were my actions so different? Had I broken a commandment or neglected a duty it would have been failure enough. But to have denied a loving relationship is beyond my comprehension. I had believed I was incapable of renouncing in a single instant the sacred, intimate associations enjoyed for several years. My self confidence turned to shameful remorse. Unconscionably, I had betrayed a friendship. He was my best friend.

At that precise moment I knew the meaning of Jesus's look. Through the prism of penitential tears I experienced, not condemnation, but undying grace. He refused to disavow knowing me, whereas I swore "I know not the man." Rather, he intended, "I know you Peter, and despite all, you truly know and care for me. You are mine, and I forgive you."

Were those eyes turned to me now I would cry aloud with passion, "Lord, you know I love you." With his help I will be held to my faith and confession, not to my denial. Lord, I love you, now and forever, for no one else has the words of eternal life.

He was certain I would deny him, yet he prayed my faith would not fail. What great reassurance for me now. He warned Judas as well, but refused to reassure him. I wonder what has become of Judas.

Barabbas: The Astonished Criminal

Sleep escaped my anguished mind mere hours before impending death. My punishment was well deserved, earned over a lifetime of run-ins with authorities. Prison had become my home; fellow-criminals my constant company. Revulsion for the now nameless police, judges and court officials flooded my memories. So too did a cry for vengeance toward the hated jailers. Their cruel, sadistic chastisements should not go unpunished.

Retribution should be meted out in practical terms—an eye for an eye. That is the law the courts used to rationalize their punishment. In the darkness brutal watchmen taunted, "You are going to suffer in the morning." And, "Get ready Barabbas, it is pay back time."

Scuffling of many feet muffled the curses of the soldiers in the dark of night, dragging a new prisoner to a cell. Hastily whispered messages passed between prisoners, naming this newcomer, the object of a mob's hatred. The none-too-subtle guards whined and complained about late night duty because of this now-disgraced Galilean Rabbi.

I could see that his beaten body appeared too weak to allow him to converse. His wounds were far too severe to promise recovery. So much blood had drained from his crushed body it now appeared to have clotted prematurely. Open wounds ceased weeping for lack of blood. I glanced quickly. I suspect he will not make it until morning. His battered face reflected endurance of a personal hell, with probably more to come.

Imprisoned fellow criminals berated him in gross verbal attacks. Naturally, I added cursing of my own, "If you are so powerful, why don't you break out of here. While you're at it, let us out at the same time." He did not respond, probably due to advanced trauma, and a body at death's door. It seemed wrong to continue, so instead I vented my hostility, directing curses toward the jailers. What did I have to lose? Execution faced me at the prison's door.

This new criminal, the one who was called the Son of God, had caused quite a stir. All-night trials such as his are rare, and accorded only to the worst law breakers. The thought crossed my mind, that if he makes it through the night he should pray for a speedy execution to put a merciful end to his incredible suffering. Rumor had it; both Pilate and Herod seemed unconvinced of his guilt. I was never given that luxury. But the mob, and most certainly the Sanhedrin, was not going to let him go. The fevered chants, "Crucify him! Crucify him!" reverberated along the fetid prison corridors.

Yesterday, in the early morning, before first light, an undertone of covert activity disturbed the fleeting slumber of the jail. Something unusual was occurring. Confused voices, painful outcries, pain-induced groans, and the thumping of trampling feet penetrated the thick prison walls. Were the inmates preparing to riot against inflexible laws imposed by prejudiced judges? My anxiety escalated. Surely my time was running out.

I heard whispered orders in the pre-dawn light, speaking of a site for executions. Three crosses were to be erected at the Place of the Skull. Obviously, one was meant for me, but what of the others? Which other criminals are destined for the most savage executions? My reverie was interrupted by purposeful footsteps approaching my cell.

As the rooster crowed I mused about the course of my life. The clank of a key in the rusty lock allowed the escape-proof door to creak open. Summoning fortitude to face the awaiting ordeal, I anticipated encountering the death squad. Instead I was confronted by the chief jailer. Though previously shock proof, now I expected the worst, but the hard-as-iron chief jailer reluctantly growled, "You are free, Barabbas. Another takes your place. He is to die between two other criminals."

Unaccustomed to the daylight, I squinted in search of some answers as I emerged from the pit. Time passed slowly and painfully as I squinted into the intrusive brightness. Were more beatings to be administered as a wake-up call? Or, hope beyond hope, had there been a stay of execution?

No one questioned the justice of my sentence. Admittedly I was a rebel against the law, a robber and a murderer. Jail was only a temporary relief. Time had dragged by slowly over many weeks as I lay bound, awaiting execution for my crimes.

Notoriety should not be equated with popularity. Though supported by those in rebellion, I and my band of renegades are not popular with law abiding citizens, but we are well known—and feared. The road to Jericho, under our protection, was a profitable venture. It was not a safe road for others to travel after we took over.

Roman soldiers were unable to quell the robberies occurring on that stretch of road. They had neither understanding nor experience in guerrilla tactics. We avoided the soldiers but saw unarmed travelers as fair game. Eventually we were out-manned, cornered and arrested. Prison time followed, with the obligatory sentence of execution. It was decided this would happen just before Passover, when the population swelled with visitors for feast days. My punishment was meant to be a spectacle and a deterrent to rebellion.

I have often heard the dreaded fear of crucifixion whispered in the prison's dungeons. Such trepidation was once distant, but surely I would soon taste the Roman scourge as preliminary to the cross. Long hours of intense agony lay on the horizon of my last day.

At crucifixion the hands and feet of victims are torn by great spikes, or trussed so tightly to a beam that circulation is cut off from the extremities, producing a fast acting gangrene. Wrists and shoulder joints become dislocated by the downward drag of body weight. Every nerve instils its own point of torture. Burning, unquenchable thirst consumes the final moments. All the while jeering and hateful mobs attempt to strike back at those who earned this fate. I anticipated that the specifics of execution would be played out as my final obituary.

I never expected a reprieve. Emerging into the glorious sunshine, I saw the crowd surging out along the Way of Sorrows, to the place of execution beyond the city walls. Who is condemned to die in my place? What offence could be greater than mine? Captured by the hysteria, I moved toward the place of execution, feeling much too conspicuous and vulnerable. I slunk down amid the crowd, eluding detection, hoping to see what would become of this criminal.

I have seen the sneers, felt the revulsion, and sensed the surprise of the crowd. Why did they stand aghast at the peculiar circumstances of the day? Courts can sometimes be soft on criminals granting early release from prison. Our land is a guerrilla country of the first order. The zealots, mercenaries and knifemen represent many groups which seek to make life difficult for the occupying forces and their Jewish collaborators. Treacherous criminals prey on their countrymen and foreigners alike. I usually took the easiest route, and the least guarded targets.

Criminals are lawless opportunists, taking whatever they can while avoiding detection. Men of blood haunted these Judean hills from the time of King David. In lands where nationalism and racial hatred burn like fire, such men achieve the status of patriots. Yesterday the leaders persuaded the mob to yell for their political victim with cynical inconsistency. Pilate, desperate to find a way out of his dilemma must have seen the blatant hypocrisy, but he took the risk and complied with the mob's demand.

Why should my name be significant? "Barabbas" is a reflection of Aramaic ancestry. "The son of the father" is a term of affection, a kind of disciple relationship to a rabbi, master or teacher. Some think I am a rabbi's son. Forget it. My name signifies nothing other than personal identity. I am struck by the irony of it. He was called the Christ, the Son of God who gathered followers to his kingdom. As a fugitive for many years I camouflaged my identity, hiding from my pursuers. I wonder now how I will be remembered.

The frantic crowd of toadies and hangers-on were after blood. Anyone's blood, so they neglected me for the moment. A small gang of friends of a formerly popular Nazarene zealot, the rabbi Jesus, was overpowered by the frenzied mob. I blended in with the furious throng.

The dispirited followers of Jesus appeared beaten and disconsolate. Their strength was gone. They had neither my experience nor zeal, and therefore were too soft, and simple. Life is not like they portrayed it.

They say that so-called bookkeeper, Matthew, called me a notorious prisoner. He should be challenged. How clean are his books, and his hands? A physician named Luke happened to be a follower of the criminal and he accused me of insurrection, and murder. My zealous rebellion is well documented, but he has no proof of murder. He had better stick to his medical texts. He does not belong to the religious crowd.

The Nazarene's confidant is a fisherman called John. He labelled me a brigand and robber, but not to my face. The tag along servant boy, Mark, is in over his head. He has been mouthing the rampant circumstantial evidence that I was a member of a gang. It's true, but so was he. Many of the curses flung at me arose from guilt by association. Was the Galilean rabbi in the same boat? His band also incorporated zealots with bloody hands seeking to throw off the Roman yoke of oppression.

Terrorists have little value in these times. Some have likened me to a bold, dashing rebel, idol of the mob, catching people's imagination with deeds of daring. Or I'm a patriot battling occupying forces on behalf of a beleaguered populace. Mine was no weak voice promoting self-denial and endurance of wrong. I will never advocate rendering Caesar's rights to Caesar. I had no challenging presence, but rather, I gave words to men's hatred and supported their resentments. The world is prone to choose its own vicious ambitions and base desires. Often the choice is fatal.

It is improbable that the priests urged my release, and even more unlikely that Pilate would grant it. Was it the psychology of the mob? I have never heard of the custom of releasing a prisoner at Passover. What goaded Pilate to affect such a rash statute for me? Desperate times may require desperate measures, but clemency was deemed impossible. Pilate's grandstanding endeavour to placate the mob was woefully short-sighted, and doomed to fail.

There are certain rare moments on which destiny turns. They chose me and rejected the Christ. When man deliberately chooses evil over good, he will reap a harvest of vile consequences. What doom awaits this nation and her leaders? What is to become of me? Will I survive on the outside of prison walls, or will I again meet the prison's pit?

Prison is ugly, degrading, indescribably corrupting of guards and prisoners alike. I hate the place. It is more detested than the pit of *Sheol* itself. For twenty years it has been my home, my life.

Life has been unfair. For as long as I can remember I received blame. Fingers always pointed in my direction and I could never win. I chose friends if they had value for my safety or escape. Friendships were fickle because there really is no honor among thieves. My life has been lived in the shadows, always looking over my shoulder for pursuers. Trouble found me wherever I hid. Nobody rescued me. It has been said "the Lord helps those who help themselves," but nobody helped me. This hell I have lived through was bound to catch up to me. Phoney lawyers and corrupt guards languish in every prison cell and hole, waiting for bribes and pay-outs. Life itself is unjust brutality.

Like me, the Nazarene was accused, tried and sentenced to die. He was not found guilty, and nothing was proven. Why then the execution? I saw him die, on a cross meant for me. Amid death throes of suffering he spoke of forgiveness, told of love, promised hope, and embodied peace. Was his punishment just? Did he receive what he deserved? My pardon secured my freedom, but at what price?

What now? I need to turn my life around. How? I am powerless. Life is a scam, a terrible fantasy benefitting a select few. No one cares, really cares for his fellow man, let alone for a lifelong criminal deserving death. Still, I saw his eyes reaching out to me, miraculously perceiving my pain. From a body battered beyond decency or recognition he spoke of forgiveness. Why?

He forgave his murderers, those whose children he had healed; the religious leaders of the nation; the military occupiers of our country; Pilate; and the mob. Why would he do this? Will there be forgiveness for me?

Rebellion against Rome is a capital crime leading to death by crucifixion. We were both condemned to die. We shared the same jail. I walked free while he took my place. His name may be translated, "The Son of the Father." Ironically, it is my name as well. Was it a fluke of fate that our paths crossed? There is much I do not understand.

Judas Iscariot: The Bitter Betrayer

Yesterday at this hour Jesus was alive. Now he is dead. They killed him and his blood is on their hands. Yet, I am not guiltless. Little did I know how bitterly my conscience would accuse me.

Thirty pieces of silver became nothing more than pocket change which I could not keep. It became a curse. My lips are blistered from my treasonable kiss. If I do not die of remorse, surely I will take my own life. It would have been a great release if only I had been nailed to a cross near his, for I too was a thief as the others beside him were, and much more. I was his betrayer, far more corrupt and more despicable than they.

My name signifies "one who deserves praise." A proud Judean am I, from the village of Kerioth, and the only Judean numbered among his disciples. Only Jesus and I trace our lineage to the most illustrious of the twelve tribes. The others are Galileans, from a province unknown in the days of our national glory. When the Maccabees walked in this city, zealots were revered; patriotism ruled the day.

I could never see why these latecomers, who usurped my position of leadership, monopolized the Rabbi's attention. His appeal was to the masses rather than a select few. None of them could say, like me, that they left home and native province to follow the Nazarene. Quite naturally I suppose, Jesus would have chosen his kingdom officials from those who gave up the most.

Like another revolutionary, Simon called the "Zealot," I associated myself with Jesus in the hope of returning Israel to her former glory. I envisioned Judah as the Lion Tribe once again.

Recognizing my talents and astute skill with finances, the

brotherhood created but one office, and named me treasurer. However, my strengths and contributions were never really appreciated. I was never given a fair shake. Sure, I took from that paltry collection bag, but they could have thanked me for the many economies I was able to manage. Why then was I always listed last? The others were grappling for positions as though it were a political gathering. Why were three Galileans selected for his intimate inner circle? Everyone was shoving for the front of the line wanting to be first. James and John, particularly insufferable, had the audacity to request special seats of honor, on his right and his left, in his anticipated kingdom. Of course I, too, coveted the honor, but not so crudely.

His "kingdom" implied Rome's overthrow. Until a week ago I fully believed Jesus had the power to rally men for this task. He had the personality and the qualities of leadership that were needed. Yet he was so young, and with little understanding of our history. Often his disrespect for our scholarly religious leaders was appalling.

It was not personal affection that drew me to the Galilean disciples. Rather, I saw the kingdom possibilities. No one in my experience was as capable of vanquishing the accursed Roman yoke. He was the man of the times, the one who could mobilize the people to wrest the nation from Roman rule. I waited my whole life for the opportunity which had been so near to my grasp.

Jesus seemed to evade the real issues. He was asked, "Lord, will you at this time restore the kingdom?"

He replied with riddles, or intimated that esoteric knowledge was required. After he fed the five thousand, they would have made him King of Israel. Instead he ignored what I believed was a more propitious time. He forsook the very people who could be foot soldiers in his empire. Why, he even gave more time to that street woman who wasted her ointment on him than to the clamouring crowds. Some thought her beautiful and sacrificing. I saw her as sinfully wasteful. He surely did not need to indulge her overt, extravagant affections, while scolding those of us who were his true followers.

The disciples' subsequent falling out with him was inevitable. He should never have censured us in front of others. I complained at the time, for the kingdom could have used the money. Giving it to the poor, who are thick as flies around Jerusalem at feast time, might have rallied more support and invaluable resources to his cause.

After raising Lazarus from the dead, a most remarkable feat, Jesus rode into Jerusalem amid crowds feverishly crying for the advent of his kingdom. I expected a day of triumph was at hand. So, what did he do? He blundered and lost the advantage. His reluctance to accept the crowd's adulation was ill-timed. His retort to the criticism of the Pharisees who were seeking to quell disorder, "if my followers keep silent even the stones will cry out", resulted in a divided city, whereby the leaders themselves assumed polarized positions of support or condemnation.

Did he not recall how earlier he alienated the hierarchy by chasing the traders out of the temple? Obviously he must have known how this enraged the high priest who had a vested interest in these things. I was aware then that the Nazarene had not a brilliant mind, rebellious heart, nor a zealot's passion.

At first I felt uneasy in Jesus's presence, for he seemed to read my motives and nature as did no other. He was different from all other leaders. More than two years ago he openly expressed knowledge of a traitor among his devotees. How irritating the day he observed, "Have I not chosen you twelve and one of you is a devil?" He could not have meant me. Nor could any of the twelve be considered demonic. When addressing us it seemed an irrelevant question.

Jesus sought my attention, my allegiance and loyalty, though on each occasion he appeared almost subversive. Mere hours ago, while girded with a linen towel, he washed our feet in keeping with our tradition. In our midst, as his tender hands touched my callused feet, he cryptically hinted, "You are clean, but not every one of you." His pronouncement was too ethereal for words. What was he thinking? What did he know?

I dared not make eye contact. I felt as though his piercing eyes could read my thoughts and reveal my very soul. Jesus instructed us to prepare for the Passover, reiterating the restrictions of the Seder according to the divine commands given to Moses and Aaron, "No foreigner is to eat of it. Any slave you have bought may eat of it after you have circumcised him, but a temporary resident or hired worker may not eat of it. It must be eaten inside one house; take none of the meat outside the house. Do not break any of the bones. The whole community of Israel must celebrate it." (Exodus 12: 43-46)

Following the ritual cleansing before the feast in the upper room he asked me to sit beside him at the table, nearer than any of the others. I was practically leaning on him. Never had we been so close. It was a special seat, an emotional moment. Why did he place me in a spot reserved for the guest of honor?

Jesus, the host at the Seder, acted according to the Passover tradition and took the sop, which is a thin wafer-like piece of bread formed as an improvised spoon to dip into a common dish, and served each of us.

When the sop was passed, a choice morsel for a favored friend, I was singled out for special attention. Could he see my face redden with guilt when he said, "He who shares my bread has lifted up his heel against me?"

Neither John nor Peter seemed to hear. Perhaps Jesus knew what I felt and believed—the kingdom was beyond him now. His best efforts had failed. It was too late. Why did he play these games? His mission, once so well articulated, was now dissipated and unrecoverable. He had unwisely surrendered himself to impotent Galilean friends.

In a subsequent dramatic moment our attention became riveted to his pained countenance when he said, "One of you will betray me." They all feigned innocence, which was impossible for me as my guilt-ravaged conscience imparted a heated flush of embarrassment. Fear of discovery produced an inner turmoil. Indigestion racked my body, giving evidence of my evil actions. Could the others read my intentions? I cringed in shame but there was nowhere to hide.

Quickly, Peter nosed in, seeking to pry inside information from John, "Ask him which one he means." My ragged breath caught in my throat as I tried unsuccessfully to respond. I knew then I had totally misjudged the Rabbi from Nazareth.

Naturally, my dreams were shattered, and completely out of reach. Either he was a reticent Messiah or a false prophet. I thought I could change his reluctance. Yet, I faced a quandary; should he be a false prophet, Moses said such were to be put to death.

There was little to lose so I devised a plan. I would be known as the man who precipitated Jesus's exercise of power leading to his elevation to the throne. Or I would be vindicated for exposing this one as a false prophet. Either way there would be no small compensation. Even the Galileans would have to give the recognition and credit due me.

Our estrangement, while never exposed, was becoming too intense. I felt he could discern my motives. Earlier at the supper his touch on my feet provoked sincere introspection. How could I do this evil? I was becoming as one possessed. When I joined the followers of the Rabbi it was without hidden motives or treacherous intentions. He could clearly see my qualities when I was adopted into the discipleship. Now I am destitute, without insight to my behaviour. I cannot account for my greed, jealousy, distrust, and spite.

I was caught unaware by the Sanhedrin. I did not expect the council to be gathered together as I entered their chamber. I had hoped only to meet with a few of the officers. Peering at the faces, flushed from the exertions of late night meetings, revealed their discomfort at my impertinent intrusion. Angrily they questioned my motives.

Though not unanimous, some of the rulers saw this as an omen to bring them good fortune. They pressured me to cooperate with their demands. I was to deliverer the Nazarene into their hands. If one or two had voiced disapproval I might have refused, but the Councilors were swift to support my role among Jesus's followers. They sealed my allegiance with a few pieces of silver. I was worth much more but they knew I wanted their encouragement, and at any cost.

I was able to marshal a large number of leaders antagonistic to the Rabbi who supported the Council's wishes. A band of soldiers from the chief priests' office accompanied me. I knew Jesus would be in the garden of Gethsemane with his remaining disciples. In the dimly lit garden there should be no mistaken identity. I led the way.

When we arrived at the garden I almost changed my mind. As we crept up to him he greeted the band and called me "friend" as I kissed him. Hot tears fell from his eyes, burning my flushed cheek. "Judas, do you betray the Son of Man with a kiss?"

My better judgment overcame that emotional contact. Those assisting in his arrest fell down, some in panic and fear, others in shock at his admission to being the Christ. For me it was too late to turn back.

I fled to the Council chambers and confronted the leaders. They feigned ignorance of the proceedings. The priests would not take back the money, though they saw how it tormented me. As I confessed my sin, I emphasised his was "innocent blood." Their own hardened hearts deafened their ears to my pleas.

Angry cursing was directed at Jesus and me, linking us together as objects of their fury. Arrogantly they stated it was my problem. They took no personal responsibility. As I threw down the coins I heard one say they might buy a field for burying the poor and forsaken. If they do I will be the first. Let me find a tree in that desolate place to hang myself. They cannot deny my place in history.

What is the origin of the Master's love and kindness? He refused to retaliate against me in the garden. I was not blamed during the trials or later, on the hill of sorrows.

I was hiding near the cross when Jesus said to the thief, "Today you will be with me in paradise." Would he say that to a betrayer? Could he say that to one who began so well and worked so hard? I wished to run and clasp his cross, and plead for his forgiveness. But that was yesterday. Today he is dead.

I tried to use him and was unable. Now I wish to find him, but know that it is too late for me. Oh, compassionate Christ, can you hear me?

Simon of Cyrene: The Brawny Conscript

It is a long way from Cyrene to Jerusalem; from the Capital city of my Country to the fulfillment of my dreams. I planned to be away from home for many days, even weeks. My friends encouraged me to make the pilgrimage, calling it the opportunity of a lifetime.

I knew it was an arduous journey, fraught with potential danger on the sea and on land. Every true believer in the God of Abraham, Isaac and Jacob longs to be in Jerusalem at Passover. I had waited for many years, and my time had finally come. My wife protested, fearing a long absence from home. I argued, "If not this year, when?"

Expectations ran high as I envisioned celebrating a Passover Seder in *eretz Israel*, as we call the land. Few of my friends are devout believers in the covenant God. Only a minority of my relatives are religious. Most of them hang on to their ethnic identity but emphasize culture and neglect faith. You would think that messages in the synagogue on feast days would prepare them to make a deeper commitment to our God. Moses exhorted in the words of the *Sh'mah*,

"Hear, O Israel: The Lord our God, the Lord is one. Love the Lord your God with all your heart and with all your soul and with all your strength. These commandments that I give you today are to be upon your hearts. Impress them on your children. Talk about them when you sit at home and when you walk on the road, when you lie down and when you stand up. Tie them as symbols on your hands and bind them on your foreheads. Write them on the doorframes of your houses and on your gates." (Deuteronomy 6: 4-9)

119

From the earliest grades in Torah school, and from synagogue worship, I have hungered to *aliyah,* to go up to Jerusalem. Cyrene gave me my spiritual foundation, but in Jerusalem I hoped to find deeper meaning in my faith. Rabbinic counselors had affirmed my desires and encouraged my initial steps of faith, approving of my determination to follow the leading of the Almighty. Rabbi Yitzak volunteered to be my guide and valet even though he has never set foot in Jerusalem. He did, however, warn me of political factions in the Temple and of a radical Rabbi from Nazareth.

Every true believer in the Almighty wishes to celebrate Passover in Jerusalem at least once in life. The Law of Moses requires us to be present at the Temple in Jerusalem and to rejoice before God.

"Be joyful at your Feast—you, your sons and daughters, your menservants and maidservants, and the Levites, the aliens, the fatherless and the widows who live in your town. For seven days celebrate the Feast to the Lord your God at the place the Lord will choose. For the Lord your God will bless you in all your harvest and in all the work of your hands, and your joy will be complete." (Deuteronomy 16:14, 15)

Throughout the school years we studied the history of my people, and the land. The two concepts were inseparable, entwined in history, from the time of God's covenant with Abraham. As part of the covenant people I was brought into the family of faith and sheltered in the covenant. I knew the people but not the land.

Initially it was a far-fetched fantasy. I wished to travel to *eretz Israel* to experience the land of my people, to taste the flavor of the culture and to worship my God in the temple. None of my family had done it, and did not see the need for such extravagance. In the early days they considered my unrealistic longings to be a wistful dream which would disappear with maturity. But it never did. I continued to harbor the hope of worshiping where our forefathers knelt, in the presence of God.

As a crossroads of Northern Africa, Cyrene embraces many cosmopolitan cultures and beliefs. My home city is ideally situated on the Northern coast of Cyrenaica, allowing its reputation as a major seaport and trading partner with seafaring nations. It was founded by the Greeks six centuries ago, and then occupied by conquering nations, including Romans and Arabs. In the Greek world Cyrene is second in size only to Athens.

Notable is the pervasive influence of the large Jewish population in our city. The many Torah schools have set a foundation for religious scholars, with education beginning in early childhood. Rabbinic students have an abundance of synagogues in which to worship and exercise their liturgical gifts. I and my family were blessed to follow the teachings learned from this spiritual milieu. For many years I dreamed of celebrating Passover in Jerusalem. The family Seders always concluded with, "Next year in Jerusalem." The time had come!

But the questions in my mind were troubling. Would Torah teaching be honored there? Were the best Rabbis teaching in the Temple? Would I discover renewed faith in the Passover? We heard news and rumors of unrest in Jerusalem, so what would I find in the City?

I traveled alone, though other passengers on board the ship also planned to disembark in the Land. Some friends who had intended to go along backed out at the last moment. Regardless, I persisted, thinking that the cruise across the mighty Mediterranean was excitement enough to make the traveling aspect of the pilgrimage extraordinary.

During the months of preparation the same questions had arisen many times. Where would I find lodging? Will my distant relatives extend hospitality? We were strangers, having never visited the other's country. Will my family be able to cope financially without my assistance during my time away? Will the weather at sea hinder my travel plans?

Voyaging on the Mediterranean Sea in the spring is usually a joy. The worst of the winter storms are forgotten as the warmer weather moderates the often fickle winds which can pipe up with little warning. Ill-prepared sailors pay an exacting price in damage to the vessel and injury to those on board. Cyrenese sailors are the best in the world, but they are no match for an angry sea. The "gods of the deep" have their way with incompetent novice sailors.

I planned for the journey by training under sail. Countless hours had seen me aboard small single-rigged dhows, learning to read the winds and the water. Out of respect for the sea I never ventured far from port. My journey to the Land carried me to the unknown, taking me across the sea and overland to the Holy City.

As the vessel bore away from shore the huge fleet of smaller boats heeled at anchor, their hulls rocking in our passing wake. The view of white-washed houses clinging to the rocky hillsides sank gradually below the horizon as we crept out of port on the local zephyrs toward the headland, where more vigorous winds would be encountered. Prevailing winds typically originated in the West, sweeping marine traffic toward Egypt and the Nile.

The captain commanded reefed sails on the two-masted schooner. The ten-man crew hurried to obey as we soon began to move north to weather before turning east toward the distant landfall. Likely, the skipper was hoping to assess the state of the sea before fully raising halyards and trimming sheets. Larger sails had been neatly flaked and stowed in sail bags below deck, waiting to be bent onto masts and forestays.

We had barely cleared harbor when the seas steepened as wind-blown waves sent spray and green water over the windward side drenching those seeking protection on the lee deck. Experience had taught the captain to respect the overpowering force of the ocean which was capable of turning on us at a moment's notice. The helm was put hard over to a starboard tack lest we got knocked down by the strengthening wind. We changed direction, and more suitable conditions propelled our ship eastward as the following wind filled the huge, billowing, off-white canvas sails on the downwind run.

Our course called for us to give a wide berth to the rugged coastline and the Nile delta. While we coveted shore-leave in the port towns we were content to view them from a distance, staying away from rocky shorelines. A ship is always safer at sea than close to shore.

Huge quantities of silt and effluent from Cairo were regularly flushed along the Nile's banks and forced out to sea. The pristine waters of the Great Sea were spoiled by the pollution from the river, pollution that could be smelt as well as seen. Brown sludge hid beneath the surface of the delta's bloom which permeated the salt water of the sea. Shoaled areas lurked underwater waiting to snag and ground wayward vessels and to correct lackadaisical navigators.

For many hours we eased along our charted course, taking frequent soundings, and altering headings as needed. With blessings from the Almighty, the consistent wind conditions and the ocean swells moving eastward from far offshore enabled us to continue toward the Land on a single tack.

A lookout high in the rigging, scanning the horizon, spotted the land of our destination later that day. But, time dragged by slowly as the light winds propelled us closer to our destination, the port of Joppa, a small seafaring village clinging to the sandy shores of the eastern Mediterranean. It was our first glimpse of the Land.

Accurate navigation brought us safely to our intended landfall, the only port between Mount Carmel and Egypt. Knowing some passengers still had three days of overland travel awaiting them did not dampen our enthusiasm for continuing the journey. On the contrary, excitement raged within me as I viewed the Land of my dreams.

The breakwater protecting the port hove into view, after which the ship ghosted along carefully making its way into the inner harbor. Line handlers received the ship's mooring hawsers, mooring us securely to the dock. Port officials inspected our papers and permitted us to disembark. I stepped ashore feeling truly lost in a foreign land. Yet, this was my land, where I belonged. I feared it would take several days, if ever, to get acclimatized to *eretz Israel* and her people.

Arrangements were made to secure donkeys as beasts of burden for the inland trek to the Holy City. Walking beside the animals was almost effortless the first day as we crossed the Plains of Sharon. But, the next day the terrain steepened as we approached the foothills beginning the ascent toward Jerusalem. It was slow going on the last day, as the increased elevation of the road required frequent rest stops.

Great flocks of fellow pilgrims clogged the paths in a disjointed parade moving toward the Holy City. The challenging steepness of the grade caused the procession to spread out as we progressed along, since most of the pilgrims were physically unprepared for the strenuous trek. I felt my weary muscles cramp with the demands of the terrain. And I had been so sure of myself when training in Cyrene. Carefully making our way along the steep and rocky Kidron Valley we arrived at the city wall below the Temple Mount. It was sundown. The setting sun glanced off the huge ashlars, illuminating these foundation stones of the Temple. That was when I understood why it was called *yerushalaim shel zahov*, "Jerusalem the golden." I was awe-struck. No doubt this would be a Passover like no other.

I discovered the home of relatives after much searching, situated in the outskirts, beyond the walls of the City of David. To my relief they welcomed me with warm kisses. Then they presented a basin and towels for the ritual of washing my feet.

We discussed the feasts and holy days with enthusiastic fervor. Worship in the Temple was to be followed by the family Passover Seder. We needed to prepare spiritually by starting with the home, preparation of which began several weeks in advance. Scrupulous cleaning was required to remove every trace of leaven. The Torah enjoins, "Do not eat it with bread made with yeast, but for seven days eat unleavened bread, the bread of affliction, because you left Egypt in haste—so that all the days of your life you may remember the time of your departure from Egypt." (Deuteronomy 16:3)

We meticulously planned the Passover meal, honoring the Torah's instructions. Of course rules of kashrut needed to be revered. For our meal to be kosher, principles from the Torah had to be obeyed. The meat must be killed in a certain way so that the blood drains away before it is eaten.

"The life of a creature is in the blood, and I have given it to you to make atonement for yourselves on the altar." (Leviticus 17:11)

Meat, whether animal, bird or fish must always be cooked and never eaten raw. Boiling and roasting are the usual methods of cooking. The Passover lamb is always roasted. Of course unclean animals are excluded as they cannot be kosher. My family insisted that when killing and cooking animals we should not be cruel to any of God's creatures. Traditionally, all these injunctions from the Torah are given as encouragements to us, so as to be spiritually ready for the Feast.

Final preparations for the Seder enjoined our preparing the Passover lamb, which according to the Law of Moses should be selected four days in advance. The Temple Mount was abuzz with merchants hawking the sacrificial lambs prepared for slaughter and other requisites of the Passover Feast. Nearby markets offered accompanying accouterments for the meal: wine, herbs, vegetables, eggs, fruit and nuts, all necessary to depict the bondage of our people and the subsequent release from Egypt. The Seder ceremony always speaks of the Passover as our "redemption."

The markets in the vicinity of the temple echoed the turmoil of the crowds. Passover is a time of restless anticipation, particularly with the massive influx of foreign visitors to the city, but certainly nothing in the past could compare to the chaos yesterday. I was told it was more than the usual Passover crowd. Something was amiss.

While still in Cyrene the Rabbis had discussed with me the politics of these troubling days. Now I was in the middle of them. A military presence was everywhere. Religious leaders were scurrying like cockroaches. Rumors of "Roman justice" flew around the Temple Mount. Posted signs warning of insurrectionists fomenting rebellion were everywhere. We were told to watch for misguided zealots.

I heard clamor and commotion from an area near Antonio Fortress, the current headquarters of the Roman Legion. It is where they process the worst criminals after their convictions. Milling crowds, appeared ready to riot at the least instigation, showing little exhaustion from attending overnight trials. Prisoners emerged amid an angry mob, rapidly growing in numbers and intensity, which escorted them along the impossibly congested serpentine roads leading from the Fort. Raucous cries pierced the explosive atmosphere. "Crucify him! Crucify him!" became a growing chant. I was stunned by the unexpected lawlessness.

What could compare to this anarchy? The great *souk* of Cairo stands alone in attracting sheer numbers of massed humanity in one place. But the Egyptian crowds seek bargains at the bazaar. What were the expectations of this crowd?

Military officers used their weapons to fend off the seething crowd. Rabid antagonists took every opportunity to inflict further torture on the prisoners. They were prodded at spear point and slashed with swords. The Nazarene, with the crown of thorns, was singled out for the bloodiest cruelties. The mob was out of control. How would this civil disobedience affect Passover?

While curious bystanders hung back in the sheltered recesses of the buildings lining the streets, more aggressive ones in the crowd shoved forward to confront the prisoners. Religious leaders and zealots nearer to the criminals joined the soldiers to intensify the physical abuse. Jesus was struck with their hard leather boots causing bloody eruptions on his shins, and savage fingers gripped his beard and tore it from his face.

Jesus had been weakened by the agonizing all-night ordeal. His ashen complexion and feeble responses indicated loss of blood. The Romans made their prisoners carry their own crosses. Some prisoners died before reaching the place of execution. Would that happen to this one? Bloody torture had slowed his reflexes, causing him to stumble under the weight of the cross. His excruciating wounds compounded the burden of the cross. His body had been beaten almost beyond recognition.

He looked nothing like the miracle worker or healer whose reputation had spread as far as my own country. Even his followers looked upon his wounds with revulsion. Disconsolate supporters, groggy from the night-long ordeal, put up token resistance and attempted to protect him from further atrocities. But it was of no avail. In the scuffling crowd he lost his footing and collapsed.

I tried to distance myself from the chaos as my emotions ran rampant. Who deserved such awful abuse? How could one, allegedly caring for others and healing the sick, be subjected to this torture?

The mob's aggression was focused on the prisoners who were

staggering toward the place of execution. Curses rang out from every quarter. Tempers flared. Many in the furious crowd pushed forward to get closer to the macabre procession. Others looked for avenues of escape. Blood-letting seemed to be the order of the day as soldiers vented their anger on any who got in their way. I tried to be as inconspicuous as possible, cowering in a secluded doorway away from the madness around me.

I tried not to be noticed but my size and darkened skin made me stand out in the crowd. I could not hide. Prying eyes of the onlookers pointed to me. An imposing armed guard rushed from the side of the prisoners. His snarling command left me with no alternative. "You," he shrieked. "Come and carry this cross!"

"Please, I cannot be defiled by blood," I futilely protested.

To do so would disallow participation in the Passover Feast, for no alien or uncircumcised person, or unclean person could partake of it. I would thus be required to undergo a period of purification. The Feast days would have passed by that time. I had traveled one thousand miles to be in Jerusalem at Passover and did not wish to be disqualified beforehand. All of my arguments came out in jumbled, nervous gibberish.

Of course Romans have no regard for our Land or for our Feasts. Soon I was surrounded by armed soldiers and at the point of their spears I was compelled into service, carrying the beam of the prisoner's cross. At that moment I could choose to be tainted by the prisoner's spilled blood or to be faced with the spilling of my own. I was not willing to sacrifice my life for the rules of kashrut and Passover. Perhaps there may be a future Passover for me in Jerusalem.

The prisoner's faltering steps confirmed that he was unable to endure further torture. Bloody wounds from numerous beatings were aggravated by the weight of the beam. The rough timber beam was saturated dark red by the blood which had spurted from his back and shoulders. My own broad shoulders soon became covered by his crimson blood.

He staggered beside me, stumbling along, struggling,

unsuccessfully, to shield his broken body from the crowd's abuse. His expressive eyes held mine in an acknowledgement of shared mistreatment. Incredibly I heard his mumbled words of encouragement to me. His faint whispers spoke of the torment he was suffering. Yet he refused to curse his captors. Jesus forgave them. I wonder if he forgave me. His gratitude brought me to unashamed tears.

Our route was determined by the surging mob as we squeezed through the constricted roads and alleys on the way outside the city wall, to the Place of the Skull. In our agonizing journey, I understood his burden to be infinitely greater than mine. My ordeal was over, but not so for the condemned one. Jesus was cruelly nailed to the instrument of death that I had been forced to carry in his place. When it was finally lifted from my bloodied shoulders I felt no sense of relief, for I had done nothing to free him from his greater load. I was concerned that I would have to miss the Passover, because I became unclean. I had sought, unsuccessfully, to avoid his blood. In retrospect, how honored I am to have been covered by it.

Our lives touched. I shared his suffering. Together we had inched along with the hostile throng to the execution at Golgotha. Then I stood with hands by my side, unable to intervene.

In the hours of darkness Jesus uttered anguished mutterings. His outcries of compassion were for others. His words of forgiveness directed toward his evil executioners indicated a supernatural love from the heart of the Messiah. I recall the admonition from the Prophet Isaiah:

"Pass through, pass through the
gates!
Prepare the way for the people.
Build up, build up the highway!
Remove the stones.
Raise a banner for the nations.
The Lord has made a proclamation
to the ends of the earth:
'Say to the Daughter of Zion,

'See your Savior comes!
See, his reward is with him,
and his recompense accompanies
him.'
They will be called the Holy People,
the Redeemed of the Lord;
and you will be called Sought After,
the City No Longer Deserted." (Isaiah 62:10-12)

Was this the fulfillment of Isaiah's proclamation? Surely, none other could compare with this one.

I came here to find meaning in the Passover by celebrating the Feast in Jerusalem. All arrangements had been made, but my participation was disallowed. Yesterday was *erev Shabbat*, the evening of the Sabbath. The family Seder went ahead as planned, without me.

While I recalled the words of our nation's redemption, integral to and recited at every Seder, the sounds and sights of Golgotha filled my mind. An innocent man, unjustly executed, died yesterday. I was unable to save him from the demise orchestrated by the unruly mob. Mutely, I witnessed the worst that evil men can do.

Could the Centurion have been correct? Was he truly the Son of God? Was Jesus the Messiah for whom we have waited? Some murmurings from his followers were heard, declaring him to be "the Lamb of God." I wonder if the many symbols of Passover prepared me to find the Lamb of God.

The way back to Cyrene may not be easy. I came to Jerusalem to find a Passover Lamb. At the Place of the Skull I saw the Lamb of God. His followers are called Messianic Jews. When he covered me with his Blood I became a completed Jew. I have changed and have been changed.

Can I say, "Next year in Jerusalem?" It is unlikely, for my life will never be the same. The emotions of *Eretz Israel* have touched my heart, but the blood of Jesus touched my body…and my soul.

Joseph of Arimathea: The Covert Follower

Why? Why did I not use my wealth to more substantially enrich his life? I have been greatly blessed by the Almighty. As in other societies, there is a strong division between the wealthy and the poor. The poor often spoke harshly of those who had money, and were wary, even suspicious of them. The prosperous were given special attention. Both attitudes speak to a sense of inequality. Wealth confers status and often people hold respectable positions in a community solely on that basis.

The Christ addressed these feelings and tried to correct them. He said money was not an advantage. In fact it could prove to be a curse. We need not envy or hate the rich, he proclaimed, for few of the wealthy would be willing to make the sacrifices necessary to enter the kingdom of God. Indeed, those who followed the Messiah had to be willing to sell everything.

Why wasn't I more "willing?" Regardless, Jesus dealt with men and women of means outside the realm of prejudice for or against wealth.

Yes, I've heard the talk. "He is a counselor of honorable estate." I thank God they do not know my heart or feel my shame. Many of these critics donated generously to the cause. My friends—Nicodemus, Zacchaeus and the affluent women—gave hundreds of shekels to the Savior. Yet, my tithes were conspicuously ineffectual, counting for little in the disciples' meagre treasury. Why have I been so weak? Why was I so insignificant in service to the Lord?

It would have been easier in the long run to be transparent. Was

I paralyzed by my fears? Oh, there would arise some immediate ramifications. My image would have been temporarily damaged. Some friends would have sought distance. Neighbors could have shunned me, and coworkers become publicly critical. Someone in my position is very vulnerable. However, they correctly guessed my secretive allegiance anyway. A man is known by his associates and his associations. If I had been painfully superficial, I might now be relieved from my self-imposed criticism.

Of course, I am a disciple of the Messiah. Were I to have my way the whole world would follow him, acknowledging him as Messiah and Master. It is proper that every knee should bow before him. Still, I am chagrined by the discrepancy between my convictions and my behaviour. My good intentions are seldom realized.

At the time it seemed right, and good, and proper. Even now I can justify my actions of subterfuge. I attempted to keep my covert actions hidden from probing critics. Without respect of my peers and contemporaries I have no audience. I believe one needs to earn the right to be heard. Some of those religious fanatics run amok with few restraints. May God deliver me from such an imbalance.

My hometown is skeptical of me. I expected more from that conglomerate of apathetic Arimatheans. Little more than a minuscule bump in the road, it is hardly large enough to qualify as a village. Just ten miles north of Lydda, Arimathea squats low on the plains of Sharon, very near the tel at Aviv. Situated in the lower foothills of the Shephalah, the spine of Palestine, it is a nondescript area known primarily as the place where Saul first met Samuel. Why were those saints brought to my memory now? I hunger for the piety of Samuel, but my performance is a capitulation of Saul. Why?

During the slavish Roman occupation my people were allowed to govern themselves. As long as their actions did not conflict with Roman laws and goals there remained a tenuous and an uneasy truce.

The supreme council which governs Jewish matters is the Sanhedrin. Its power depends greatly on the personality and courage of the council in session combined with the current attitude in Rome. Our decisions influenced Judaism throughout the world. We patterned ourselves after the group of elders called by Moses to govern Israel; elders to share the burden of ruling the people. Sadly our history is not one of grandeur.

Herod the Great, appointed by Augustus, decided to reorganize the Sanhedrin. When he came to power he executed the ruling officials. Jesus might still be alive were it not for that murderous lunatic. Herod's cozying up to Pilate was an alliance certain to bring about the demise of the Nazarene.

Today the council is comprised of Sadducees, Pharisees, high priests, heads of tribes called elders, and legal authorities called scribes. A total of seventy make up the body with the reigning high priest acting as chairman. The council sits in a semicircle in order to see each other. Two clerks record proceedings and count votes. Only twenty-three of seventy are required to be present to hold court. If the accused man was convicted, more council members could be summoned to hear subsequent arguments in the case.

There can be no doubt the Sanhedrin exercised rightful jurisdiction at the trial of Jesus. His crimes were of a religious nature. Thus the council had the authority to call him to account and render a verdict. Perhaps some technical rules were violated. It is thought we erred in disallowing proper clothing, but his behaviour was contrite and respectful. Still, I am dumbfounded by one inescapable breach; there was no fair attempt to ascertain his guilt or innocence. The guilty verdict against Jesus was rendered without a single dissenting vote. How was that possible? Nicodemus, a respected member of council, must have been absent, as was I. I know not his reasons, and I am unsure of my own motives.

Was it cowardice? Weakness? Fear? Unpreparedness? In retrospect, my vote was irrelevant to the outcome. Ironically it is a matter of paramount significance now to me. How deeply I long to revisit the decision of the council. Alas, it is too late.

In ashamed silence I endured the shouts of praise the day after the Sabbath. My duplicity troubles me more today than ever before. He was the Messiah! David's Psalm prophesied:

"Many bulls surround me;
strong bulls of Bashan encircle me.
Roaring lions tearing their prey
open their mouths wide against
me.
I am poured out like water,
and all of my bones are out of joint.
My heart has turned to wax;
it has melted within me.
My strength has dried up like a
potsherd,
and my tongue sticks to the roof of
my mouth;
you lay me in the dust of death.
Dogs have surrounded me;
a band of evil men has encircled
me,
they have pierced my hands and
my feet.
I can count all my bones;
people stare and gloat over me.
They divide my garments among
them
and cast lots for my clothing.
But you O Lord be not far off;
O my Strength, come quickly to
help me.
Deliver me from the sword,
my precious life from the power of
the dogs.
Rescue me from the mouth of the
lions;
save me from the horns of the
wild oxen." (Psalm 22: 12-21)

As read the text I was blind to the reality of his Messianic identity. Even after I learned of him I missed the truth of my personal lack of courage. How could I have stood by, immobile and unspeaking, merely a mute observer? Why could I not respond to the Savior? Where was my praise?

My silence condemned him. Further, it condemned me. My own emotions betrayed me. Tears erupted, blurring my vision. My eyes, filled with adoration and love, gave evidence more compelling than my contradictory body language. "Even the stones will cry out," he said. Yet I spoke not. God, forgive me. Today, I am beyond his forgiveness.

The philosopher, Socrates exhorted, "Know thyself." You see, that is my problem. What I know is not what others surmise. I am given deference. They murmur, "He's a good and righteous man." "He looks for the kingdom of God." It has even been intimated, "He was Jesus's disciple." Perhaps. But it was only when condemned by my own introspection that I was reluctantly goaded to action.

It came to me during the traumatic procession. I feared to approach Pilate, lest he see through my feigned bravado. I had been reticent too long. I was inexorably prodded by my guilty conscience. My resistance to becoming identified with the Master, finally broke down.

We, Nicodemus and I, took that precious body from the cross at Golgotha. I tentatively touched his mortal wounds. His heart was deathly still. A ghostly pall emanated from his lifeless body. What horror! I shall never again see such unspeakable suffering.

We prepared for his burial, not with preservation in mind, but to allow the body to naturally decompose. Generous amounts of costly perfumes and spices were placed inside the wrappings to control odors. As well, we applied seventy-five pounds of myrrh and aloes. These preparations were meticulously carried out in consideration of my love for the Master and in sympathy for the expected guests who will customarily visit the tomb within the first year. They should not be overwhelmed by the aura of the cemetery.

The tomb was an inheritance from my immediate family. It had never been used. I considered it an honor to have my own body, one day, interred next to the Galilean. We rolled a large stone across the entrance to protect the corpse from scavenging animals and grave robbers.

Following the Sabbath I will go back, along with the women, to complete the preparation of Jesus's butchered body. I wonder how we can remove the stone. Pilate's paranoia about Christ rising on the third day is absurd. The stone itself is obstacle enough. And then to post a group of guards. Why? Surely, that is unnecessary.

My life—what is it now? I would trade places with him if I could. Now it is too late. Why was I so insular, so ignorant, so selfish, so guarded, so silent? If only I had spoken in the council meeting! If only I had protested at Golgotha! If only I had unreservedly proclaimed the Christ!

If he would walk away from that grave, I would serve him with my life—without ever asking why!

A Centurion:
The Converted Executioner

I watched and reflected while surveying the execution site. It was at times like this that I knew I was a soldier.

Decades of preparation, training, hopes and dreams provided my current select status. I recall the schools, military academies and camps. Instructors were harsh, demanding obedience in each lesson. A premium was placed on perseverance. I strove to the head of the class. It may have been my destiny. My father and his father traced their military roots down through the past five generations; soldiers, centurions all. It is in our blood.

Much of my success in the ranks stems from physical talents. I am blessed with the keen eyesight of an eagle, the marathon-like endurance of a camel, the heart and strength of a lion. Equally important are the intangibles that comprise my bearing; mental balance and wise judgment and add a touch of daring.

Along the chain of command my name is admired. Strength plus stamina along with determination brought many promotions in rank. I am a soldier. Look at me. My family is proud of the honors bestowed upon me. Sadly, I've been overlooked for certain postings. Why did the gods ordain duty in this bleak, austere country?

I worked for Herod Antipas. That assignment should count for something. Though the Jews were always leery of him—he was half Idumean and half Samaritan with not a drop of Jewish blood in his veins—I respected his firm hand, and he acknowledged my military leadership. Herod's gross immorality was overlooked by my men. His private life should be kept separate from his public rule.

In contrast, the crucified one might still be alive today had he turned a blind eye to Herod. Similarly, radical John the Baptist confronted Herod's sinful practices and it cost him his head. But since Rome assigned him the tetrarchy of Galilee, I will abide by the Emperor's political judgment.

What was it like when my father served the Emperor? Will we ever return to those glory years? In those days flag and country were revered and the military was feared at home and abroad. Now we are regarded as lowly as the civic police. How pitiable. You can't go back, and I personally will never retreat.

Still, it is galling to be so linked with these unpredictable Jews. They are aloof yet wanting, no, demanding their way and identity. They absolutely refuse to accept our better technology, advanced learning, international experience and superior lifestyle. They will not abandon their past. Why not? Their history is littered with fanatics and false messiahs.

The power of our nation is the military, and the strength of the military is the chain of command. Central to all is the role of the Centurion, a commander of one hundred men in the Roman legion. Our ordinary duties are to drill the men, inspect their arms, food and clothing, and to command them in the camp and in the field. We are employed at times in detached service somewhere in the provinces. We fear these assignments. There is no telling when a crazed group of zealots will foolishly take-on the invincible power of Rome. As luck would have it, we are too often caught in the middle, between the government and the guerrillas.

The duty section from the garrison at Antonio Fort, inside Jerusalem's wall, is a brutal lot. It is not without reason they are resentful of this stint of duty in a tense Jerusalem. Yesterday's events escalated the tensions and may trigger a horrendous explosion among the unstable mobs. Throughout Palestine our Roman legionary walks in perpetual fear of the terrorist's knife or zealot's dagger. Pilate's irrational leadership has filtered down the ranks. Fear runs rampant.

Centurions are a necessary, moderating influence in this hotbed of tensions. Picked for our military manner, the Palestine garrison was additionally chosen for its toughness. Revulsion of Jews is an additional asset, hence, the childish but sadistic mockery in the barracks room, and the cruel crown of thorns. The brutal punishment pleased the curious crowd which endured the trial proceedings and subsequent execution. Some chose to jeer and mock the criminals, whereas others joined in with physical abuses of every sort. Crowd control became a priority, as the unruly blood thirsty mob desired to become vigilante executioners before we arrived at the Place of the Skull.

The prisoner was wildly acclaimed as King of the Jews last week when he arrived in Jerusalem. He had more advanced publicity than me. Last week my men were warned by the religious leaders to be on the alert, guarding against a possible riot. Sunday's march was uneventful aside from a few boisterous supporters. Afterwards the scene changed as later, he was denounced, arrested and charged in a Jewish court according to local law.

I am not sure why blasphemy is so significant to the Jews, but it doesn't matter. When the Jews brought the prisoner into the Roman court, they claimed he was a seditionist. This is one charge the Roman government takes seriously. Once the prisoner was in the custody of our courts and subject to our great judicial system, he became my responsibility.

I was just doing my job, following orders which are passed along the reliable chain of command. Though uneasy with the punishment I was watched by the shouting crowd, so I pummeled him from trial to trial. Punches and body blows were witnessed with shouts of approval.

Somehow each encounter with the judiciary seemed like a travesty of justice. The final indignity was when Pilate submitted to the deranged mob. Would I have ruled otherwise? Crucifixion is extreme, and these Jews understand little other than force.

Romans are not particularly compassionate when viewed from the perspective of an occupied country. My government has long adopted suppression as a means of control. We know these Jews hate Roman occupation but it is a necessary expedient. They are a rebellious people, strong willed, and difficult to govern.

Centurions typify all that is distasteful about Rome. We have become the brunt of Jewish aggression. Regardless of their distaste for our presence, most people respect us for bringing law and order to this frontier.

One other vital role we play: the Jews have no death penalty in their courts. Apart from Roman rule they must deal with hardened criminals according to their own weak laws. Pilate waffled, attempted to pacify the mob and then gave him to us to execute, all of which is legal under Rome.

We crucified him at Golgotha, a place infamous for intense suffering and death. On a hill outside the city I sat down and watched. My men carried out the decreed punishment. One of them drove the huge four-sided spikes through his wrists. While not unique, it was contrary to the usual practice of tying the condemned to a cross. I continue to be astounded by the many "irregularities" of this execution.

Then they all sat down below the agonized figure of the crucified one and rolled dice for his cloak. Another soldier was entrusted with the task of smashing the legs of the three crucified men. This practice prevented the frantic lifting of the body on the nailed feet as the victim struggled for a few precious gasps of air. Though weakened to the point of death, the strained, uplifted chest made breathing excruciating. The victims would therefore die more speedily of suffocation. I have seen much suffering, but cruel torture is distasteful to me.

One of the band of soldiers in a gust of pity had driven his spear into a sponge, used no doubt to wipe blood from his own hands. Subsequently he dipped it into a jar of sour wine which stood there and offered it to the Christ.

Whoever swung the sledge hammer to break the prisoners' legs abstained when he came to the convict for he found him already dead. Roman soldiers are very familiar with death. We know a dead man when we see one. Was this a sensitive soldier who for some reason hesitated to maim a corpse?

We acted for Rome. A death sentence was carried out. Though never pleasant, occasionally executions are warranted. On the hill of sorrows we saw the most amazing event in all history. It was surely the most awe-inspiring spectacle set before the eyes of men. It was both tragic and a travesty, yet the most glorious deed ever performed on earth.

To these soldiers it was an ordinary day. Criminals are often crucified as a consequence of their actions. We have carried out similar executions hundreds of times. But I saw this one strangely different. We observed this man, the crucified, voluntarily laying down his life for the very ones who had forfeited every claim upon him. I believe the man on the cross was the Christ.

My vision and hearing were alert to what I saw and heard. It was unlike any previous experience. Yet, I know what I witnessed.

He confronted his mother as he died. That she even appeared at the site was remarkable. Parents are noticeably absent in courts of law, let alone at a scene of execution. It is as though crime is contagious, or shame too wide-reaching. Further, he comforted John, one of his closest friends. In spite of unspeakable agony he conversed with the thieves going so far as to assure one of them of heavenly rewards. All along his followers murmured promises about the Kingdom of God, citing Jesus's warning,

"Watch out that no one deceives you. For many will come in my name, claiming, 'I am the Christ,' and will deceive many. You will hear of wars and rumors of wars, but see to it that you are not alarmed. Such things must happen, but the end is still to come. Nation will rise against nation, and kingdom against kingdom. There will be famines and earthquakes in various places. All these are the beginning of birth pains." (Matthew 24:4-8)

The crucified one, the one nailed to the cross, tried to respond but only halting words escaped his fevered lips. During those hours an intimate transaction took place between God and the crucified one.

I know not the content of his prayers. His body seemed to betray his mind and will. In contrast to every execution in my experience he did not protest his innocence, nor did he scream obscenities at my men.

He did not curse the ones who cried for his blood, those who approved as he was nailed him to the cross.

Instead he comforted those around him. To the end he proclaimed his doctrine of love, saying "Father, forgive them." His death touched my life. That moment was infinitely too sacred for human eyes to gaze upon; a mystery which no mortal minds can completely comprehend. He made a sort of covenant about which he had spoken and which was sealed with his blood.

Coincidentally, I heard the veil in the temple was torn in two. I felt, and dreaded the earthquake. Rocks were hewn in pieces. Graves mysteriously opened. If he was the creator of heaven and earth, then heaven and earth expressed their sympathy in these powerful signs.

In the treatment he received we observed sin in its true colors, stripped of all disguises, exposed as rebellion against him. At the cross I saw the climax of sin. He hung there as the sin-bearer for all who believe in him, even other criminals. Jesus received the punishment due all men, especially me. As I watched him die I reflected on my own life. He took my place!

Some will hear of his death yesterday and think, no doubt, their attitude toward the crucified one is a matter merely of negative indifference. I say to them, "You err." If you are not a friend you are an enemy. He reportedly said, "He that is not with me is against me." There is no third classification—and no appeal. If we despise his authority and refuse to be ruled by him then we are united with those who hounded him to death. He reportedly prophesied, "The sun will be darkened and the moon will not give its light; the stars will fall from the sky, and the heavenly bodies will be shaken." (Matthew 24: 29)

At midday we could no longer watch him, for it became as midnight. Perhaps nature itself was mourning such a sight. When I witnessed the things that were done I feared greatly. All-pervasive dread captured my being. I dared not restrain a compelling cry, "Truly, this was the Son of God."

How will I be seen and judged? Will I be cast as an obedient Centurion, simply but dutifully following orders, as is my career and calling? Or will I be considered inhumane for the spear I allowed to be thrust under his rib cage, emitting the outpouring of blood and water? It apparently was the spear that revealed the damage to his lungs, and the traumatic pleurisy occasioned by the merciless scourging. Some will honor my allegiance to Rome and my respect of our code. Regardless, I have been loyal to my unit, the forces and my country.

At the time of his death three great world powers were joined on this desolate desert hillside. Over the cross, above his body, I read, "This is Jesus, The King of the Jews." The script in Hebrew, Latin and Greek represented the language of religion, of government and of culture, respectively. Each of those forces signified opposition to the crucified one.

I know both what I saw and whom I saw. My deepest desire now is to show them all what I believe. If he meant what he proclaimed, "Father, forgive them for they know not what they do." I will see him again one day. Maybe I am the first of the gentiles to accept the truth of his life. Tragically, I witnessed, indeed abetted, his suffering and death. Meanwhile, I will wait, hope, wonder, and watch.

CRISPY WINTERS & UNBROKEN SHELLS

by Amanda Kroll

My name is Amanda. *Crispy Winters & Unbroken Shells* is the heartwarming story of my childhood experiences with epilepsy, divorce, the death of a friend, first love, and lasting friendships.

From my first memory—playing with roly-polies on the sidewalk—to the unbearably hot day I received my college degree, this creative memoir is filled with colorful memories covering the span of twenty years.

Crispy Winters
&
Unbroken Shells

Amanda Kroll

Paperback, 108 pages
5.5" x 8.5"
ISBN 1-4241-9861-5

About the author:

These experiences, along with the wonderful relationships that have developed between myself, my mother, my twin sister, and my baby brother Ram, have molded me into the quirky individual I am today.

Don't Praise Me, Praise God

by Shirley Edwards

It's time to put God's will first in our lives and live for the Lord. Some pastors are focused on members, money and the luxurious lifestyle. "If you have the members, you have the money; if you have the money, you have the luxurious lifestyle." How can someone lead you when he or she is doing wrong? Also, we need to search God for ourselves and ask Him to give us understanding. Many things have changed in life, but I know that God has not changed His word. Man has made things suitable for his own purposes. Also, many pastors are preaching for the wrong reasons. Their luxurious lifestyles have taken their mind off the important things of what the real meaning of serving God is. God knows our hearts and He knows a true leader. Having a fancy car, fancy clothes, and a fancy home—what good are they when your soul is not right with the Lord? When you step out of God's boundaries, there is no hope without repentance. People need to take control of their lives and let "God use them."

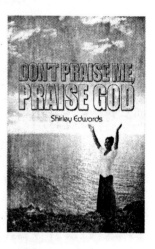

Paperback, 90 pages
6"x 9"
ISBN 1-60563-181-7

About the author:

As you read this book I hope that you will be encouraged. I do believe that *Don't Praise Me, Praise God* will be one of the most talked-about books that has ever been written. May God bless you all.

COPS, DONUTS, AND MURDER
by George Galjan

A police pursuit turns ugly and the suspect is shot to death. The community is up in arms. The coroner and the police forensics team conclude that it was an accidental shooting. However, the FBI believes otherwise. The officer involved turns up dead. Is it murder or suicide? Crew members from the tugboat *Bufford*, which included the son of Cleveland's mafioso, turn up dead in various parts of the city. All this awaits newly promoted Lieutenant Pavlick and his partner Sergeant Fu Chu Lai. When Sergeant Fu Chu Lai was shot, by of all people, the FBI, a newspaper columnist blamed the incident on donuts, and published an article, "Why Cops Crave Donuts." The following day the police were overwhelmed with donuts, and...

Paperback, 283 pages
6"x 9"
ISBN 1-4241-4284-9

About the author:

George Galjan was born in 1942 in Berlin, Germany. In 1956 he immigrated to the United States with his family. After high school, he enlisted in the Navy. He served two tours in Vietnam and later transferred to the Navy Reserves. He retired from the Reserves with the rank of senior chief. In 1969 Galjan joined the Cleveland police department. He retired in 1998, holding the rank of lieutenant. He currently resides with his wife, Margaret, in Avon Lake.

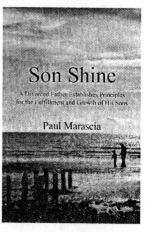

Also available from PublishAmerica

WHEN MOMMY WAS A SOLDIER

by Fran E. Orr

Maggie is very proud of her mother. She and her Nana sit together looking through a photo album of photographs of her mother's life. Maggie asks Nana to tell her again why her mother joined the Army. She learns about the values and strengths that make her mom a winner.

Paperback, 26 pages
8.5" x 8.5"
ISBN 1-4241-9576-4

About the author:

Fran E. Orr is married to a retired naval aviator. Their youngest daughter served almost four years in the Army. You will enjoy this story of a young woman's choice to serve her country as seen through her daughter's eyes.

Available to all bookstores nationwide.
www.publishamerica.com

Also available from PublishAmerica

VERTICAL BLINDS
by Stefanie L Plaud

Poetry is pain, identifiable, raw and unpolished. *Vertical Blinds* is like a heart sliced into four chambers: anger, jealousy, resignation, and hope. Each section is a tomb, a dedication to stages of life that are in a constant card game, shuffling for position. These poems are a calling to those that feel the darkness coming, and don't have the words to expose it. The cult of beauty is outdated, and these words—gritty, exposing, sometimes brutal—are a window into a trapped mind, reaching out to those who feel the same. They are not alone.

Paperback, 63 pages
6" x 9"
ISBN 1-60672-899-7

About the author:

Stefanie L Plaud is a 2006 graduate of Roger Williams University's Marine Biology program. She currently works at the University of Maine's Center for Cooperative Aquaculture Research. *Vertical Blinds* is her second book. *Rib Tunes*, Plaud's first volume, was released in 2005.

Available to all bookstores nationwide.
www.publishamerica.com

DESTINY OF A WAR VETERAN
by Sal Atlantis Phoenix

Destiny of a War Veteran depicts the life of a conscientious veteran. The subject matter of the story is serious and tends towards the realistic side of the aftermath of war. The story is about the analysis of the human soul lost in fantasy and in reality, about submission and rebellion, and about philosophy and tyranny. The story is vivid with images, and complex and rich in characters. It is an intriguing tale that defines the socio-political scenarios.

Vietnam War veteran Joe is tempted to participate in Middle Eastern and international politics, compelled with insinuated illusion of establishing

Paperback, 188 pages
5.5" x 8.5"
ISBN 1-4241-8005-8

freedom and democracy. The subsequent effects of the human tragedies engulfed from the political scenarios devastate him, and he seeks refuge beyond the realm of humanity.

About the author:

Sal Atlantis Phoenix, a veteran of life and a conscientious citizen, is a playwright and fiction writer. His lifelong experience convinced him that "…with all its sham, drudgery and broken dreams, it is still a beautiful world. Be careful. Strive to be happy."